AFRAID OF THE LIGHT

An anthology of crime fiction with
a foreword by Alex North

Rachael Blok
Heather Critchlow
Elle Croft
James Delargy
Clare Empson
Jo Furniss
N J Mackay
S. R. Masters
Phoebe Morgan
Dominic Nolan
Robert Scragg
Victoria Selman
Kate Simants
Adam Southward

'We can easily forgive a child who is afraid of the dark; the real tragedy of life is when men are afraid of the light.'

PLATO

CONTENTS

FOREWORD

I'm writing the foreword to this book at an extraordinary time and in an extraordinary place.

The time is Saturday the 4th of April, 2020, at which point my country is in the grip of coronavirus. That means we're effectively in lockdown, and I'm confined to my house, so the place I'm writing this from is my living room. Now – don't get me wrong here – I like my living room. But it was not designed to handle this lack of traffic, and over the past few weeks it has grown over-familiar to me, increasingly off-kilter and strange.

A bit like life itself, I guess.

I find it odd to think that a century from now the children of our children will be studying this period of time in their history lessons. They may well focus on numbers and statistics, but the most obvious change for me is the loss of contact. Human beings are social animals, after all, and right now we're all adjusting to a new world of talking to each other over the phone or in a video call, of smiling and nodding to a stranger across the street, of shouting conversations across a fence from a safe distance, or down the queue outside a supermarket. Because the thing is, we're human, and that's what we do. We are – all of us – full of life, and of stories that demand to be shared.

Not all stories are real, of course, and it seems to me that fiction is particularly well-suited to these days of social distancing. Somebody far smarter than I am described fiction as an act of telepathy: a writer, with an image in their head, describes it in

words; and then a reader, interpreting those words, receives that image in their own head – as if by magic. Crime fiction, to me, feels especially geared towards making sense of the world around us. In this volume, you will find stories by fourteen brilliant writers. The stories are wildly entertaining in their own right, of course, but they also address the concerns and fears we all feel: isolation and loneliness; guilt and grief; justice and punishment. And perhaps most importantly of all: redemption and hope.

Which brings me to the Samaritans. The flipside of having stories to tell is that you need someone there to listen to them. Well, that is what volunteers for the Samaritans do. Every minute of every day, every day of every year, people volunteer to answer calls from people, all of whom have stories to tell, many of them very sad stories indeed. And whatever story you have to tell, the Samaritans do something extraordinary. They will not judge you; they will not offer advice or tell you what to do; they will simply listen to you. And no matter what you're going through, over the course of that phone call, you will know that you are not alone.

That's the least we all need.

I hope you enjoy the stories to follow. I started by saying we were in an exceptional place, but I think the fundamentals remain the same: we have stories to tell, and we need people to listen. By purchasing this collection, you have helped. Keep reading, I reckon. Keep hearing, absolutely.

And most importantly of all, keep listening.

Stay well and stay safe,

Alex North, April 2020

CONTRIBUTORS

Are you Listening? - Adam Southward

Daddy Dearest - Dominic Nolan

Deathbed, Beth Dead - Elle Croft

Loveable Alan Atcliffe – S R Masters

Sleep Time - Phoebe Morgan

Coming Home – N J Mackay

Sausage Fingers - Victoria Selman

Just a Game - Rachael Blok

Drowning in Debt - Heather Critchlow

To Evil or Not to Evil - Jo Furniss

Sheep's Clothing - Robert Scragg

Frantic - Clare Empson

Planting Nan - James Delargy

Shadow - Kate Simants

ARE YOU LISTENING?

Adam Southward

The blue light pulsed. Ready. Listening.

'I don't understand,' I said. 'Why would she make something like this up?'

Laura shrugged, hugging her arms to her chest, staring at the kitchen wall, at the red brush strokes scrawled across it. 'She was adamant. It told her to.'

'It is just a microphone and... software.' I peered at the innocent white cylinder, perched on the edge of the kitchen worktop. The shimmer of the LED was captivating. The potential fascinating. Always on—that was the promise. Always ready.

Harmless.

'I don't know why we bought it,' she said.

'It's fun.'

'It tells you the weather, James.'

'It plays my music, controls the lights. It's... useful.'

'It told our daughter to write that,' said Laura, pointing at the wall.

The words were scrawled, harsh and vivid, drawn with a child's paintbrush, the brightest red, the most violent of language.

'It listens to everything we say,' she added.

'Nonsense,' I said, struggling to understand where my seven-year-old daughter had learned such hateful things. My precious Ava: gentle, caring, never before uttering such words. 'She's obviously been sneaking onto Netflix, watching something horrible. Perhaps your laptop?'

'My laptop?' Laura looked unimpressed. 'James, look at it. This isn't funny.'

She was right. I looked for a light-hearted spin on it but found nothing.

'Where is she?'

'In her bedroom, crying,' said Laura. 'She said the woman's voice told her to write it on the wall. That it was a warning. How does it know her name, James?'

I let out a long breath, realising I'd been hunched over with tension. My shoulders ached, and my confusion remained. This was out of character for Ava, using language I didn't think she even understood, let alone knew how to spell. If she said she heard it, then...

'Let me check,' I said, remembering that the device kept a log of everything it heard in the app. I scrolled through the day's entries, past the morning radio, the news, the inevitable weather request. I'd used it to check my emails earlier, but nothing had been logged in the last couple of hours, least of all something related to the blood-red message of death that adorned our dining room.

'Anything?' said Laura.

I shook my head. 'It must have been the TV. Or a dream.'

Or a memory... I shivered. Not impossible, but unlikely. She was too young, had been too young.

I turned to face it, human against machine in some ridiculous stand-off. The blue light never wavered. I cleared my throat.

'Computer,' I said. I'd changed the wake word—it let you pick anything, but I'd chosen the geekiest option. The blue light flashed. 'What was your last command?'

A pause. Pulses, spinning.

Then the light went out.

I'm sorry, it said. *I don't understand the question.*

3

◆ ◆ ◆

I heard Laura shouting. Saturday morning, a week later. I was in the bathroom, enjoying a leisurely shower. My next shift wasn't until late Monday. The shout repeated—urgent, painful. 'James, come down here.' I grabbed a towel and sprinted downstairs, stumbling at the bottom, stubbing my toe against the floorboards.

'Fuck,' I hissed, hopping into the kitchen, unprepared for what I saw.

Laura stood in the centre of the kitchen, hands shaking as she struggled to hold Peter—our lop-eared bunny—who was kicking out, panicked. Wide-eyed, his white fur was stained red at the neck, down onto his chest.

It took me several moments to take in the rest. Ava stood to one side, face streaming with tears, her shoulders heaving with silent sobs. On the floor between Laura and Ava was a kitchen knife, the blood evident on the blade and handle, a trail of drops towards Ava, her yellow dress and hands smeared.

'What...?' I stepped forward, reaching out to take Peter. Laura's eyes were full of warning. She shook her head, small quaking movements as she passed the trembling animal over.

I examined Peter as best I could. It was just a nick on the throat, enough to soak his fur, but the bleeding was already slowing. Laura passed me a fistful of kitchen towel and I held it against the wound.

'Ava,' I said, crouching until my face was level with hers. 'Ava, what happened?'

Ava's face screwed up in anger. 'It's not my fault!' she shouted.

We'd bought Peter six years ago, not long after we got back from Europe. Ava was still a baby, but she adored the sight of him, staring at the small ball of fluff as it hopped around the garden. I'd never seen Ava so much as raise her voice towards him.

Peter kicked out and I let him go. He hopped into the corner, stayed near the fridge, watching us.

4

'I didn't say it was your fault,' I said, taking her small shoulders in my hands. 'But you must tell me what happened. Why is Peter bleeding? Why do you have blood on your hands?'

Ava shook her head. 'She said I had to.'

I frowned, glanced at Laura.

'She?'

Ava's eyes darted up to the worktop.

I followed her gaze. The white cylinder remained silent, pulsing orange as I watched it. The light spun twice, then faded. The familiar blue shimmer appeared.

I shivered. Ridiculous. Nonsense.

'Darling, I don't know what you mean. It's just a...' I pointed to it. 'A—'

'She said I needed to practise.'

Ava's tears had stopped, but her face was resolute.

'She said what?' I asked, not believing it. Not for a second. Once again, I pulled out my phone, opened the app, searched the history. Nothing. The assistant hadn't been used all morning.

I glanced at Laura and shook my head, before crossing my legs, getting more comfortable on the hard tiles.

'You think somebody told you to cut Peter? To hurt him?'

Ava nodded, small jerking movements. Her whole body was trembling.

'You heard it in your head?' I was suddenly full of dread. Perhaps I was wrong. We had no idea, not really. What deep psychological issue would cause such violence? Animal cruelty was symptomatic of so many psychiatric disorders, my head spun with the gruesome possibilities. My poor Ava. I held her tight against me, waiting while her trembling subsided.

'How do you turn this off?' said Laura, approaching the worktop.

I glared at her. 'It's not the bloody voice assistant, Laura.'

She looked unconvinced. 'Just tell me,' she said, then without waiting, pulled the power cable out of the back. The blue light flickered twice before fading to nothing.

Laura crouched, the three of us awkwardly huddled on the

floor. The daylight seemed to fade, my weekend mood evaporating in a whirlwind of worry.

I could see Laura struggling. The graffiti was one thing, but today we'd stepped into frightening territory. What were we facing? What had we done?

'Why are you switching it back on?' Laura frowned.

'Don't be ridiculous,' I said, waiting for it to power up. 'You heard the therapist today. This is not the problem, Laura.'

We were nervous about taking her; of what might come out. But everything was in order, and we had no choice. We couldn't let Ava suffer. She was our miracle.

Whatever voices Ava could hear were coming from within, that much the therapist was certain of. The cause of them was a work in progress, but our initial assessment concluded that we should proceed with therapy sessions spread over the next few weeks. Ava had been quiet and polite throughout. Puzzled, she'd responded to all of the questions that Dr Moltom had posed, shrugging when asked what the voice in her head sounded like.

'I'm not allowed to say.' After that she clammed up.

It was Laura who'd mentioned the voice assistant. I saw the therapist's eyes, her scribble on her notepad. She dismissed it.

'If Ava doesn't know, then she's likely to pick the first thing she sees.'

The weeks rolled by; the summer waned. Things didn't improve, but at least we'd begun to clarify them.

At the second session, the therapist asked Ava to draw her house, the people in it, the things that made her happy, and the things that made her sad. I can't have been the only one of us to see the small red circle in the kitchen. Ava scrawled it with coloured pencil, round and round. Spinning.

'I'll get rid of it,' I said.

The therapist made another note. She caught my eye and shook her head. 'Don't. I don't want to change her surroundings.

Leave it as it is.'

The third session wasn't until next week, so we headed home. My stomach churned with worry. Laura's eyes flashed with guilt.

I slipped my arm around Laura. Ava ran out of the kitchen, upstairs to play.

'She'll be fine,' I said. 'We'll be fine.'

Laura shook her head. 'I'm worried, James,' she said. 'I thought we'd get an answer. A diagnosis. I thought it would be...'

'More exact?'

'Precisely.'

'She's only seven,' I said. 'You can't stick a label on her issues that easily.'

The tears welled in her eyes. I held her tighter. 'She's not supposed to have issues at her age,' said Laura, sniffing into my neck. 'This wasn't supposed to happen.'

We couldn't know what would happen. We went into this with our eyes open. I thought we had.

'What if it's buried?' said Laura. 'What if it was from before?'

I held her tighter. Before? Ava couldn't possibly remember. She was too young.

I was convinced Ava was simply going through a difficult phase. In my career I was used to watching people, their reactions, their emotions. While I couldn't dismiss Ava's actions, I told myself they were temporary.

'Computer,' I said. 'What's the weather going to be like today?'

The blue light flashed, spun.

Today, she said, *the forecast is changeable.*

I drifted, daydreaming, staring out of the kitchen window, juice in hand. The run had done me good. A few blocks, nothing more, enough to clear my head, and enough to tire me out to the point my thoughts wandered.

I heard Ava's footsteps behind me, her sneakers padding across the tiles. She stopped. I turned.

She used both hands to hold the gun. It was heavy, my revolver, and it wavered in her grip.

I swallowed, placing the juice slowly on the worktop. My heart flipped and thudded, my eyes darted over my angel. Her face was rosy, flushed, her eyes wide, her jaw clenched.

'Ava,' I said. 'Where did you get that?'

I kept my revolver locked in the safe in our bedroom. It never came out until I was ready for work, and it went back in the moment I returned.

Ava remained silent. A single tear rolled down her left cheek.

'Give the gun to me, Ava,' I said. There was six feet between us. I could lunge, probably grab it before she had a chance to fire. Probably.

Ava shook her head.

'I can't,' she said.

'Yes, you can,' I said. One step forward. Ava took one step back. Where was Laura? The house was suddenly quiet. Just Ava and me.

I stared at the barrel. My mind whirred. The safe combination was known only to me, but I'd left it on the default. Emailed to me by the manufacturer. My email. My account.

A flicker of uncertainty. My eyes darted to the white cylinder on the worktop.

I use it to check my emails.

The blue light pulsed, gentle. Harmless. Nonsense.

'Please, Ava,' I said. 'Give me the gun. This isn't funny.'

'I can't,' she repeated.

'You can,' I said, my voice rising. 'Because I'm telling you to.'

'Don't tell me what to do.' Her grip faltered for a second, but she adjusted it, lifting the gun higher. I could see her finger on the trigger. The safety was off. How was that possible? I'd always shielded Ava from the guns. She shouldn't know how to do this.

'But I'm your dad, Ava,' I said. I took another small step, shuffling forwards. Still too far to be sure I could grab the gun without danger to either of us.

'No, you're not.' Ava's voice changed—deeper, mature. I didn't recognise it.

I paused. 'Not what?'

'My dad.'

The words hit me with such force I staggered. Our eyes met. I saw damage, grief and ruin. I'd seen it before. Many times, but never in a child this young. Never in Ava.

'Don't be silly,' I said, but my voice betrayed me. I stuttered, trying to form words that might bring her to me, away from the brink.

Ava gulped. Another tear, then several, streaming down her small cheeks. 'I have to do this,' she said.

I shook my head, cold fear creeping down my spine. I saw no way out. 'You don't have to do anything,' I said. My voice squeaked; my heart thudded.

'Yes, I do!' Ava shouted, her small body shaking. 'She said I had to. She knows!'

Nonsense. Crazy. I refused to believe it.

Nobody knew what Laura and I had done.

'She told me,' said Ava. Her tone was fragile, her immature voice breaking with the effort. 'She said I could go home.'

I glanced between Ava and the kitchen worktop. I stared at the innocent piece of technology, the plastic-covered circuit board and speaker, the microphone that waited, scanning the airwaves for an opportunity to wake up, to contribute. To listen to our demands, send them into the ether where an artificial intelligence made sense of them, made a decision, made a judgement, formed a response. Listening, always listening. Laura's repeated warnings; too little and too late.

'This is your home,' I said. 'It's always been your home.'

Ava shook her head.

'You're a liar.'

The truth hurt. I thought of our many hushed conversations, Laura and I, late at night, early in the morning. It was something we lived with, something we could never share. We only had each other to talk to, and that was our burden. We'd convinced ourselves we had no choice.

It listens to everything we say.

My realisation was worthless.

I turned to my stolen daughter.

'Ava, I—'

I heard a final click as Ava pressed the trigger.

The white cylinder remained motionless, the microphone trembling with the sudden soundwave. The light spun, switched to red for a split second, spinning, connecting, thinking. It struggled, cycling through until it was satisfied. Balance restored.

Red to Amber.

Then it flashed blue again.

Ready. Listening.

Adam Southward

Adam Southward is the Amazon bestselling author of TRANCE, PAIN, and MIRROR (coming September 2020). He is a philosophy graduate with a professional background in IT, working in both publishing and the public sector. He lives on the south coast of England with his young family.

@adamsouthward

https://www.amazon.co.uk/Adam-Southward/e/B07NQNXLLG/

DADDY DEAREST

Dominic Nolan

Roache was shoeless, tin of Special Brew in one hand and shirt in the other, when he cut the queue in the chippy—that point of etiquette turning into a misunderstanding that cost the aggrieved party a good chunk of ear.

Figuring in for a penny in for a pound, he took his leave by way of an alley out back, and three doors down went on to take twenty thousand quid and a useful amount of mobility from a woman closing up her bureau de change. He'd gone out for a fish supper and come back with just about everything that was possible.

He knew they'd string him up for the robbery and for the two counts of GBH. He knew best case scenario by the time they let him out he'd be older than anyone he knew in the whole world. Knowing all that, he didn't tell them where the twenty grand was and they told him he could do the thick end of fourteen years.

He didn't care.

With his previous stints and the foster home before that, he'd been inside one way or another for more years than he hadn't. What he knew best of all was how to do time.

What he didn't know was more than ten years later he would be transferred from the lifers' nick to a Cat B local, where he'd meet Miles Baron, doing a sixteenth year for murder, and fall a strange kind of in love with him.

A kind of strange that takes the earth from under your feet.

The orderly in laundry, ex-navy man name of Mitchell, took an instant shine to Roache, who had run the cleaning in his previous place. Saw him as an old hand with years in and a few more yet to go, someone he could trust for a while. Someone he could leave in charge of the private wash.

Working the machines wasn't a task any man wanted. Prison-issued garb came in and went out randomly, you never got the same stuff back. Sometimes the hot water was on the blink, or there was a shortage of powder. This, when half the clothes that came in were smeared in shit and cum and piss, was a biohazard.

For those inmates who could pay, laundry was collected from their pads and brought back ironed and neatly folded. A lucrative side-business for any decent orderly.

Baron could pay, he was well-positioned for a con. Older, in his late-fifties, and something of a celebrity—the renowned barrister who stove in his wife's skull with a granite mortar. Popular among inmates, he offered advice on how they should defend themselves in adjudications, though never raised the hackles of screws by defending anyone in person.

Roache had delivered Baron's wash a few times, usually with an audience hanging in the door to his pad, but it was when he found him alone making tea that they first spoke.

'Cardamom and ginger,' Baron said, without looking up, sensing Roache watching him.

'I know. Wondered where you got fresh ingredients.'

Baron looked up, frowned a little before smiling. He poured two cups.

'I feel I know you.'

Roache glanced down the wing. 'I don't think so.'

'No. I know that I don't. I'm saying what it feels like.'

He sat on the only chair, by the table at the back of the cell between the two beds. With his finger he pushed one of the cups over to the edge, then put his glasses on and went back to the crossword on a folded newspaper.

Roache sat on the bed nearest the cup and peered at the tea. Bits floated in it. He'd never had it that way, but in that place of all places he wasn't averse to new things. Took a sip and put it back down. Figured maybe he'd drink a bit more, so's not to be rude, but Jesus Christ.

Baron drank from his. He spoke again without looking up, something he did a lot, Roache would notice.

'Had a housekeeper would make it like this. Except not like this. I could never get it quite right, even though I watched her do it and did everything identical. I think she was a witch.'

He worked at his crossword. Roache sat quietly. He could hear voices humming in neighbouring cells, not enough to make out.

He finished the tea.

◆ ◆ ◆

Then there was the day Shufti died.

Roache had been promoted to the enhanced wing after three months. There was less churn in the population there, and better facilities. He'd had to do three months in standard before he'd been considered, but kept his head down and made sure he didn't get noticed for the wrong reasons. He'd needed to get on that wing, get away from the lip-flappers and the teeth-gnashers and the night-criers, away from those men likely to make him hurt them.

Not long after that he became Baron's pad-mate, his old one getting released. Very quickly they were comfortable with each other. Having done enough time, they both knew how to see it out, knew how to handle staff without becoming screw-boys or grasses. They could spend their locked-in hours together quietly, reading or watching TV (when someone's kettle didn't blow all the fuses). They both knew when the other wanted to talk, or when they didn't—had no need to bridge silences with their voices, eyes, egos. Their routines were simple and complimentary.

Shufti was different. Restless, in a constant moil, he found it difficult to settle anywhere. Barely five foot and built like a toothpick, he'd done a couple of holidays for burglary and was on remand awaiting trial for grievous bodily, the details of which Roache just couldn't see the boy doing.

He was having a few issues with a group of cons, his pad-mate mostly, a weightlifter called Clyde with big shoulders and narrow teeth. Liked making a point—the one chair in the cell was his when they ate, and since the bottom bunk was his too, Shufti had to sit on the khazi which didn't have a lid.

Clyde was the sort of con who made Roache long for being back in a lifer nick. Roache's old governor told him his transfer was a reward, ten years of good behaviour getting him a spot in medium security. Truth was, he preferred Cat A. Most of them were lifers and everyone got used to each other. Got older together, shared the same problems, didn't have anything to prove.

Cat Bs had a transient local population—prisoners on remand before trial, or housed for a couple of weeks awaiting sentencing, or just after sentencing seeing where they'd be sent longer-term. It was always the young ones caused the trouble. These boys in for cars or drugs, everything was front with them.

That was Clyde and his mates, and the staff weren't doing too much as Shufti had form for complaining about every little thing. Nothing changed even after he was found curled up on his bed bleeding into his sheets. Bit of a patch up from healthcare, back to his cell to recuperate. For days he refused to come out, which got him nicked and scheduled for adjudication.

He made another complaint about the assault but the paperwork mysteriously disappeared, the chasm between the official record and reality in prison never wider than it was with sexual assault. Shufti was told he was being transferred, the effective way of shutting up any con. Next evening he never showed after dinner for a meeting about his transfer, and when Baron went to see where he was he found the lad hands-in-his-pockets hanging from his bunk by a ligature made out of his joggers.

Roache had never seen Baron shaken like that. He barely spoke for days, until one night Roache awoke to him shuddering with muffled sobs in the other bed.

What can be said about those pads? Small enough during the day, even if you had a southward-facing window and the door open, at night they cocooned you with your own miseries. Roache got up quietly, sat on the chair. Sniffed to let Baron know he was there, before putting a hand on the other man's shoulder. Baron let it stay there. Calmed down some.

A good pad-mate wasn't essential, but it helped. The best Roache ever had were all killers, from his first who had watched his girlfriend bleed out after chopping her arm off with an axe for putting sweetener in his tea instead of sugar, to his last in the lifer establishment, who had shot people for money, including an Edinburgh gangster with his wife and two children. Prison treated all cons the same. Unless you were put on numbers for being an ex-copper or a nonce, it didn't matter what you'd done, you all had to abide by the same rules, deal with the same boredom, look at the same four walls over sixteen hours a day. A good pad-mate was a pal. They got you through.

Baron pulled himself up, sat with his back against the wall. Roache eased onto the bed beside him, sensing nothing was required of him beyond lending an ear.

'My Tommy, he used to make coffee first thing. Was always up early, even in his teens. I'd come down and sit at the breakfast bar in the kitchen and he'd have a cup ready. Day I found him, I sat there like usual but couldn't smell a pot on the go. There was a mirror on the wall, and from the stool I could see back into the living room round the corner. That's where he was.'

Roache had heard stories about Baron's son, but they'd never spoken about him before.

'He'd used one of the ceiling beams. Feet couldn't have been more than a foot off the floor. They're untidy, the dead. It had run down the inside of his legs and dropped off his runners onto the wooden floor. Wasn't until Jeannie came down and saw him, wasn't until she screamed that it felt real. I was sat there as if someone was still going to make me coffee.'

Their feet hung out over the side of the bed and they watched them carefully. After a while, Roache moved his hand, maybe to hold Baron's, or pat his thigh, squeeze his shoulder, something. But Baron defended himself with words.

'I have cancer.'

'What?'

'It's fine. They'll cut it out and it'll be fine.'

Grief moved him the way wind does winter's tree, and he allowed it to overtake his wariness. Heaping his pillow and blanket against Roache's thigh, he dropped his head there like a battered boat washing up on shore, holed and empty. Roache reached out and lightly, with the tips of his fingers, stroked the rim of his ear. Baron fell asleep.

Thinking it quite ridiculous, Roache was glad to be needed.

Summer disheveled them.

Lying narrowly on one bed or the other, if not embracing then at least in contact. Their breathing in rhythm, their thoughts uncluttered. The pads were hot, the nights damp like something you wore—pearls of sweat blistering on those parts of them that touched. Pillows creased, sheets rode up.

For a while there was nothing more than that, nothing more than a need for the other to be there in the sapping heat. Tussling with the nights, they dozed here and there and when they found themselves unable to sleep, they sometimes chatted and other times did not. During one such comfortable silence, Roache's tight boxers betrayed the manly state in which he had awoken. Baron put his hand there, as if it was something he had done every night, through the fabric gently milking it top to bottom, and soon it was something he did every night.

Outside the pad they gave no indication of what they were to each other, sex between inmates not being prohibited but romances between cellmates a sure-fire way of getting moved to a different wing. Having gone under the knife and had his prostate removed, already the size of a horse apple before the malignancy, Baron wasn't up to favours being returned. Though he was a free man once more when standing over the khazi, truth was he was a little too free occasionally and was embarrassed by his incontinence.

◆ ◆ ◆

Autumn was bridled by a late heat, the muggy air cloaking every movement.

Once a month, every month since he'd been locked up, Baron's sister visited. Unable to reconcile this wife-killer with the boy she grew up with, she packed those thoughts away and had over time transformed their relationship into habit, something she did with the turn of the calendar come rain or shine, until she no longer remembered things had once been some other way.

Roache had no family, had no visitors. A solicitor in the early days for the usual business, and a woman from a charity once. It came to him as a revelation that he had nobody he might call friend who he hadn't met within prison walls. So when a visitation request arrived from Hep, a former pad-mate at the lifer prison, released after twenty-two years, he accepted greedily.

The visiting room was busy. Seats were in fours, welded to metal bars like crosses around a too-small and too-low table, and bolted to the floor, like a school dining hall designed by someone who had never before seen humans. Hot drinks and snacks were served through a small hatch in the wall, including a selection of chocolate and crisps that maddeningly were not available through the prison canteen.

Hep, who everyone said had hepatitis C but was actually named Heppenstall, was three years from his pension and breaking his back picking iceberg lettuces on a farm in the Fens.

'Perfect marriage. No other bugger'll do it, and I can't get any other work.'

Munching lesser-spotted confectionary, Roache listened contentedly to his friend telling him about the tractor-pulled production line that followed him and his fellow workers up and down the neatly ordered rows of lettuce, and stole glances at Baron across the large room. His sister had her back to Roache, but she seemed just how he had imagined—tall, strident, taking control of this alien space she found herself in every four weeks.

He hadn't meant to see or be seen by her, but his farewells with Hep were shorter than those of a brother and sister, and he walked by them on his way back to the wing. She made such a noise, lowing like distressed cattle, that everyone turned to see. Roache thought at first something had happened, her heart or an embolism or some sudden affliction, but she pointed directly at him and screamed. When Baron touched her arm she batted it away and slapped him in the face. Staff got involved and the room was cleared. Emptied of people, the fixed chairs resembled jacks in a game of knucklebones nobody could win.

It was several hours before Baron returned to the pad.

Roache stood up from the bed. 'All right?'

Baron nodded.

'Your sister—?'

'I told them that I'd hidden my cancer from her and she got upset.'

'What did happen?'

'Told her about us. It's taken her long enough to get used to me as a murderer, especially as she and Jeannie were close. The idea of me with another man—'

'She'll get over it?'

Baron shrugged. 'Said she's going to stay away for a while.'

Roache stood at the window. Between buildings, the sliver of green they could see had rusted with leaf-fall. Baron came up behind him.

'Not your fault.'

'I know.'

Roache felt Baron's arms snake round his hips, his joggers loosening as the tie was unknotted. Turning him round, Baron knelt before him, the hard floor chastising his knees like church stone.

◆ ◆ ◆

A quiet year passed.

Spring arrived unheralded by winter and the summer air was slow again, before thin autumn gave way to another unpromising winter. Roache believed himself ageless, face and body marked now only by the teeth of decades rather than seasons or years. Baron's sister never returned.

With that way time had, the day arrived of miserable and happy fate—Baron was transferred to an open prison in readiness for his eventual release. The powers that be, having considered his spotless record inside, along with the unpremeditated nature of his crime and the weight of his son's death upon his mind at the time, deemed him fit to re-enter society.

For many weeks after he left, Roache resented him bitterly. Baron was a killer and now a traitor, and Roache knew only he could love him and not the outside world. One night he took a lot of pills and his new pad-mate woke up to find him unconscious, but the prison doctor saved him. Suicides were too much paperwork, so the incident was never remarked upon and wouldn't impact upon his own prospects for release.

Letters from Baron went unanswered but continued to arrive unabated. He was back in his house that his solicitor had maintained for him. He had redecorated. He wanted Roache to come stay with him when he was released.

Possibility festered in Roache's mind, the dream more alive than the cons who surrounded him, more real than the four walls that held him. He craved the long prison nights so he could crawl off and be lost in his sleep with the promise of the thing.

Near the end, he spent nine months at an open farm prison and boiled eggs in his kettle for breakfast. They grew vegetables and ate them but had no new books. Word got to him that Hep had passed away, and Roache tried counting the number of friends he'd lost within walls or to the unbearable liberty that followed, but ran out of fingers. He swam in the dead, got drunk on them. They'd never see or talk or breathe or live again, and from inside his pad Roache wasn't sure he would either. When no one was looking, he touched them to his lips. He couldn't get enough of the dead.

Freedom was a felled tree. It looked like it used to but was silent, inert, something to be climbed over. He took a train to the twenty grand in cash that had cost him his parole, still buried where he'd bundled it up in a shoebox. But they'd changed the money again whilst he was gone, some conspiracy to ruin him, the bastards leaving him with wads of withdrawn notes whose existence he could hardly explain to a bank in order to exchange. This would have been a good story for the chaps inside, this would have been something to dine on for weeks. He resolved never to tell a living soul, though Baron didn't count.

Shoebox under his arm, he made his way to his friend's house and it scared him more than any prison ever had. Nothing that big, that free, came without a cost. Waiting for him out front in a dressing gown, Baron looked old and weak.

'The cancer's back. A different cancer, they say, but what are the chances?'

It was early, but they had drinks and cheered themselves up by setting light to wads of stolen cash on the rear terrace and tossing them up in the air, fluttering down around them like burning angels.

'We must make plans,' Baron said, and Roache nodded gleefully, having never made a plan in his life. Baron would go under the knife a second time, would give him power of attorney, would write him into his will since his sister had yet to show her face again, and Roache agreed to it all with the profound certainty none of it would come to pass.

Baron faded quickly in the early evening and Roache helped him upstairs. They lay on his bed as free men, capable of coming and going from the room as they saw fit. Freedom was a yawning chasm, however, and Roache stayed where he was—with Baron's head on his chest he ran one thumb lightly round his ear like he used to, the other between his toes looking for jam. He felt like someone else, like a stranger to his own listing imagination. He could see the sharp edges of the world so exactly but make out none of its facets, like holding something dark up before the light.

That was when he saw it, when everything revealed itself to him and he knew.

Knew why Baron's sister screamed.

Knew why his wife got her brains beat in.

Knew why his son hanged himself.

'That's your boy, over there.'

'The photo? Yeah, that's my Tommy.'

Knew there was always a cost.

Couldn't tear his eyes away from it, the frame on the dresser and the face of the young man held within. It was so uncanny, he could have been looking in a mirror, could have been looking at a picture of himself twenty years earlier. So completely did they look alike, Roache and Baron's son, he doubted a father would have told them apart at the same age.

Or any other age, even if they were now distinguishable by death.

Dominic Nolan

Dominic Nolan lives in London, where he wrote PAST LIFE and AFTER DARK.

@NolanDom

https://www.amazon.co.uk/Dominic-Nolan/e/B07QBMZ5T4

DEATHBED, BETH DEAD

Elle Croft

I fight back a sob as I peer into his eyes, the blue of his irises shrouded at intervals by drooping, papery lids. He'd be more comfortable if he was sleeping, unaware of the pain coursing through his suddenly fragile body. But, because I am selfish—and because without him I will be completely alone—I'm desperate for him to cling to consciousness, no matter how painful it is. If he closes his eyes, if he gives in to the battle against oblivion, he may never come back. And, in the end, I'd prefer for him to be the one in pain, not me. I can't do it. I can't survive grief like that again. So yes, I am selfish.

Selfish. Self-aware. I'm many things. But I'm not an orphan. Not yet.

Doing my best to block out the mechanical beeping, the smell of industrial-strength disinfectant, the squeak of shoes on the linoleum hallway, I try to focus on the man whose body is stretched out in front of me. If I squint, and ignore the sounds and smells around me, I can almost imagine that we're back in the house I grew up in, that I'm bringing him breakfast in bed, the way I used to every Sunday as a child. The idea of being back there—of being happy again, in that carefree way that I was, once upon a time—should be alluring, inviting.

But it has the opposite effect. I'd never go back, not in a million years, not for a million pounds. Because after that happiness, I know what happened next.

The man on the bed sighs, and my memories disappear like wisps of smoke. With effort, he peers at me.

'Honey,' he croaks. I grab his hand, then loosen my grip, fearful that I could be hurting him.

'Dad,' I say, almost choking on the word. 'Dad, please hold on. They've said there's still something they can try, an experimental surgery. Please don't give up.'

He shakes his head, almost imperceptibly.

'Sorry, baby girl,' he whispers. 'I'm doing my best, but...' he trails off, licking his cracked lips. I look around for water, then lift the cup to his mouth, my hand shaking.

'You're doing great,' I say, hoping I sound convincing, knowing I don't. 'I'm just sorry I couldn't get here sooner.'

The guilt that hit me as soon as I hung up from that awful phone call is perched somewhere at the top of the mountain of grief that's threatening to crush me. When I allow it a moment, I know it'll all come hurtling down, an avalanche that will break my bones and turn me inside out. It's not like I live abroad, or that I don't see him on a regular basis. I'm an hour away. We have lunch every second Sunday.

And yet, I didn't know. I didn't see the signs. The nurses tell me I couldn't possibly have known what was happening behind his ribs, but their assurances do nothing to ease the sense that this is my fault, in a vague, and somehow still all-encompassing, way.

'Baby girl,' he says, interrupting my thoughts. 'There's something I have to tell you.'

It's clear by his tone that he thinks this is goodbye. Goodbye. Good? Whoever called it that had clearly never really, truly said it. I swear I hear my heart tearing down the middle, splitting apart right here in a hospital room where no one can fix me, where no medicine can put me back together again.

'No, Dad. Save it until after the operation. I'll be here.'

'I won't... I can't, honey. I have to tell you. I have to...'

His face—which seems to have hollowed and aged overnight —crumples, and I freeze. I've never seen him cry, not even on that morning all those years ago when he woke up and discovered that our lives would never be the same again. Through it all, he was stoic. For me. But not anymore. Our roles have reversed. His tears flow freely, while I remain stone-faced, desperately trying to be strong.

'I'm so sorry,' he stutters through his tears.

'You don't have to be sorry, Dad,' I say, my tone urgent. 'You've been the best dad that I could ever wish for. Just you and me, mac and cheese. Better together.'

'Mac and cheese,' he smiles, remembering the nickname he gave us after Mum's funeral, when we clung to each other for dear life, unsure how to carry on.

'But I have to tell you,' he insists. 'I... I'm not who you think I am, baby girl. It was me.'

'What do you mean? What was you?'

'Your Mum. It was my fault.'

I frown, squeezing his hand, his words squeezing my heart.

'No,' I say firmly, wondering whether the sickness is affecting his memory as well as his lungs. 'It's not your fault. There's nothing you could have done. No way you could have known, Dad.'

Even as I say it, as I repeat the words that have been said to me so many times over so many years, I know how he feels. I blame myself, too. Of course I do. Why hadn't I heard the intruder? Why hadn't I protected her? Logic would suggest that I couldn't possibly have fought off the mystery man who battered my beautiful mother on the staircase three days before my seventh birthday. On the rare days when I allow myself some kindness, some compassion, I know that this logic rings true. Even the best detectives were baffled, I remind myself. They never found the murder weapon, never understood a motive. They never even really had a suspect.

Beth Peters is the kind of unsolved case that gets wheeled out every few years for the true crime fans to chew on, for forums to come to life about, for me to fall apart over.

And it's the same thoughts that haunt me, every time. I should have protected her, saved her. Or, at the very least, I should have solved her murder, brought her killer to justice. So I can only imagine how my Dad, a man with power in his muscles and protectiveness in his bones, must feel.

'You don't understand,' he cries. He's sobbing now, and it scares me. I've never seen him like this. 'I killed her. I'm a murderer.'

I look around frantically, desperate for a nurse. He doesn't know what he's saying. This disease is taking his mind as well as his body.

'Shhhh,' I try to soothe him, but he won't be calmed.

'I was so angry,' he says, his voice quiet now, simmering. 'She was having an affair. I loved her, but she betrayed me...'

I'm staring, trying to understand his words. He's not making any sense.

'No, Dad,' I say. 'You don't know what you're saying.'

'I did it,' he repeats. 'I killed her. I hid it. It's under the floorboards in the kitchen, under the fridge—'

'Mr Peters,' a nurse interrupts my dad's nonsensical ramblings, her cheery voice jarring against the strange atmosphere that has fallen over us. I'm still staring at him, horrified, searching for a spark of mischief in his eye. It's a terrible joke, but it has to be a joke. Doesn't it?

'I'm sorry, Miss Peters,' the nurse says. I look up numbly to see a tribe of medical staff surrounding the bed I'm sitting beside. 'The surgeon just arrived. I'm afraid we have to take him in right now. It's the only chance he has.'

I nod, unable to speak or move or think. Hands press gently against my shoulders, and I'm moved across the room, out of the door, into the waiting area. I cry. I comply. I watch as my Dad's body is wheeled past. His eyes are closed. The nurses are running now. There's yelling, and more squeaking of shoes, and then I'm left alone in silence with an invisible fist around my heart.

Once again, I didn't get to say goodbye.

◆ ◆ ◆

I sit heavily on the floor, panting from the exertion of moving the fridge by myself. I can't remember how I got here from the hospital. All I know is that I have to know. I have to see with my own eyes so I can reassure myself that he's not guilty, that he did the best he could. I'm angry at him for being sick. Angry at the sickness for taking his sanity and making him think he's a monster. Angry at myself for not saying goodbye properly, for not telling him what he means to me.

The nurses told me they couldn't promise anything.

'Hope for the best, but prepare for the worst,' they'd said. As though death was the worst.

I prise a floorboard from its resting place with a screwdriver, not bothering to be gentle, not caring how much damage I do. My heart plummets into my stomach, winding me, as the board comes loose and reveals a space, the width of the floorboard, gaping up at me. I can't breathe. I want to go back to two hours ago, to when Dad and I were mac and cheese, when I looked at him the same way I have done since I was small, like he was my hero.

Reaching my hand into the chasm, my fingers brush a solid object. Part of me expects a rubber chicken, or a note from my dad telling me that he got me, a sick joke made by a sick man. But as I curl my fingers around whatever's down there, I know it's neither of those things. My mouth goes dry. I lift whatever has been buried here, the heft of it echoing somewhere deep inside me, into the light.

As the hammer, covered in flakes of something so dark it's almost black, swims before my eyes, my phone rings. I answer it mechanically, not caring what happens, lost in my father's dark truth. Carrying his deathbed confession.

'Miss Peters,' says the pleasant voice. 'This is Jane Aggarwal, I'm a nurse at St. George's Hospital.'

I try to ready myself to react. To be the grieving daughter. To say goodbye to my hero, in more ways than one. To pretend he was the man I always believed he was. To write a eulogy that skips the truth, that glosses over his cowardice. I know I'll never be ready. And once I get over his death, I know I'll never get over his life.

How could he be the man who killed my mother?

How could this be true?

An affair. Dad had said that Mum was having an affair, that he'd been angry. But the police never found evidence of infidelity.

They'd also never found the murder weapon, although they did suggest that it could have been a hammer, or some other type of common household tool.

The steel head stares back at me, taunting me, daring me to face the facts. How could Dad know that this would be here, unless he was telling the truth... Unless he had killed my mother?

'...paperwork later today,' says the voice in my ear, and I try to focus, my stomach convulsing dangerously. I haven't heard anything she's been saying.

'I'm sorry,' I whisper. 'What did you say?'

I can't deal with this right now. I can't say goodbye to my dad, while also trying to understand whether he was a murderer, as he claimed. Do I go to the police? Do I tell them what he said, get the hammer tested for DNA, find out whether that's my mother's blood flaking off the surface and onto the wooden floor?

Or do I preserve my father's memory? Let him be the mac to my cheese, remember him as the man who got me through the worst time of my life... The man who may, in fact, have caused it?

I want to scream, to run, to escape whatever atrocities—casket selection and wreath arrangement and photo printing—that will inevitably follow this phone call. But I breathe in, rolling my shoulders back, holding the hammer in front of me as though it will give me the strength I need to battle my way through this.

'He survived the operation,' the nurse is saying, and my heart cracks open once again.

'No,' I whisper, for entirely different reasons than those the nurse assumes.

'I know. It's a miracle, love. He's going to be fine.'

There's a pause as the weight of her words rests heavily on my shoulders, on my conscience. And then she speaks again.

'It's an absolute miracle.'

Elle Croft

Elle Croft is the author of top 10 Kindle bestseller, THE GUILTY WIFE, as well as two other psychological thrillers, THE OTHER SISTER and LIKE MOTHER, LIKE DAUGHTER. When she's not writing, she works as a freelance social media specialist and blogs about travel, food and life in London. Elle co-hosts the true crime podcast Crime Girl Gang, along with Niki Mackay and Victoria Selman.

@elle_croft

https://amzn.to/2X3vOsO

LOVEABLE ALAN ATCLIFFE

S R Masters

Loveable Alan Atcliffe: that's what they call him.

Like Mrs Montgomery, who waited for the breakdown people for nearly an hour in the dark of winter 2001, before Alan pulled over in his taxi and changed her tyre in just five minutes. Or Father Chase, who knows Alan was the secret donor of the final £2000 that the church needed to pay for a new roof.

Loveable Alan Atcliffe, who lives in the cottage out on the green, behind the school and the duck pond. Some people in Balsall Common would go further; they would use words like virtuous, or perhaps even saintly. People like Mrs Donovan, whose mother timed her heart attack to coincide with the terrible snow of 2006.

Mrs Donovan's car became stuck, and when she tried to dig it out her snow shovel snapped in two. She tried fruitlessly to dig with her hands, and was on the cusp of giving up when Alan's taxi lit up her drive and the man himself stepped out.

'It must be my lucky day,' she said.

'God doesn't do luck,' he replied and gave her a snowy-white grin. 'Morris Danner told me he saw you struggling out here.'

He began to dig but soon realised the true extent of Mrs Donovan's plight. Throwing down his shovel, he said, 'I'm taking you to the hospital myself.'

'Alan, you can't take me to Shrewsbury. That's nearly sixty miles. You can't.'

But he could and he did, and when she tried to pay him the fare that racked up on his meter, he refused to take it.

Loveable Alan Atcliffe.

Mr and Mrs Baines will tell you about Alan, too, and they are better placed than most to do so. In the rainy summer of 2005 their only daughter, Verity, went missing after her piano lesson. She was a beautiful girl, with bright blue eyes and long yellow hair. Some in the village, those who had watched her gliding down the streets like she owned them in the last year, secretly feared the worst.

Of course, it was Alan who helped organise the first local search party. Dressed in his Wellingtons and his brown Mackintosh, he banged on every door to drum up numbers. Then he led a team of nearly forty men and women from one end of the village to the other in the last hours of daylight. Mr and Mrs Baines had never expected such a response when they first knocked on his door to ask if he might have spotted Verity on his travels.

As if these efforts had not been enough, he took a central role in making sure that Verity's name stayed in the general public's minds once the national media grew bored of the story. He helped the Baineses build a campaign website to keep her memory alive and even donated the first funds to aid a private investigation into Verity's disappearance.

On Christmas Day 2006, not long after the big snowstorm, the Baineses invited Alan to dinner. As the pudding and brandy burned in the centre of the table, Mrs Baines turned to Alan and asked, 'Be honest with me. I know you will. Do you think she's still alive?'

The others assembled were silent. Alan placed a tender hand on Mrs Baines' shoulder and looked into her hopeful eyes. 'I believe she is. And I pray she is.'

Mrs Baines tried to smile but cried instead. Mr Baines came to hold her but she was already in Alan's arms, which, although she would never tell Mr Baines such a thing, was her preference.

Loveable Alan Atcliffe, that's what they call him. Every man, woman and child in the village: Loveable Alan Atcliffe.

Of course Alan is a humble man, and he would never think of himself as loveable or saintly. But he understood why some thought of him that way. It was because they had not seen what Alan had done in the rainy summer of 2005. The thing that only the Lord Jesus Christ had been a witness to.

Alan had been lazy that day. He had not turned on the back wipers of the taxi. A harmless enough evil, and one born of a righteous belief that summer owed him a rear-window view. As he backed out of the drive—a thoughtless, automatic act—he assumed the way was clear, because it was always clear, and it was only in the daytime that the children came past on their way to school.

It was a fact of the everyday: the girl should not have been there.

But she had been and the Lord Jesus Christ bore witness silently as the car first knocked Verity Baines to the ground, and then ran over her head as she lay unconscious. Alan remained silent as he pulled at his hair and tried not to scream as he first caught sight of the awful mess running down his drive from beneath the car.

'What were you doing there?' Alan asked the girl as he placed her in the boot on a pile of old newspapers and black bin bags.

The Lord Jesus Christ had no need to reply. God didn't do luck.

Loveable Alan Atcliffe.

Who cried as he cleaned his drive with a snow shovel and a hosepipe.

Who dwelled upon his reputation and his standing in Blythe for far too long, and had to buy a large steel container from the DIY shop.

Loveable Alan Atcliffe.

Who once a year places a bouquet of flowers in the corner of his cellar, before kneeling down to pray on the concrete floor he put down just as the rainy summer of 2005 came to an end.

S R Masters

S R Masters is an internationally published short story writer and novelist. His short fiction has appeared in venues such as Shock Totem, Lamplight, The Fiction Desk, and the Press Start to Play anthology.

His debut novel, THE KILLER YOU KNOW, a coming-of-age murder mystery set in the village next door to Alan Atcliffe's, was published in the UK by Sphere/Little, Brown, and in the US by Redhook/Hachette.

@srmastersauthor.

www.sr-masters.com

https://www.amazon.co.uk/Killer-You-Know-Original-gripping/dp/0751570362/ref=tmm_pap_swatch_0?_encoding=UTF8&qid=1585823497&sr=8-1

SLEEP TIME

Phoebe Morgan

My son has always been frightened of sleeping.

When he was born, he cried a lot. My friends reassured me—all babies cry, Laura—and I could tell that they thought I was being a bit precious about the whole thing. But I knew. This was something more than the usual new-born screaming; my son was afraid. And I didn't know how to help him.

Fast forward to when he was five. My husband, James, was working longer and longer hours, leaving me alone with our little Flynn. I got into the habit of pouring myself a glass of Malbec, sitting beside Flynn's bed, stroking the damp curls of hair off his forehead until his breathing slowed and sleep settled around us. When I was sure he'd nodded off, I'd creep out of the room, stand in the hallway for a minute, my shadowy figure illuminated in my son's doorway. I used to focus on his little chest, watch it rising and falling, rising and falling. I guess you could say I was a bit obsessive, but then, we're all obsessive about the people we love.

Downstairs, every night I'd try my luck—keep the TV on low volume, sink into the sofa—but without fail, every night Flynn would wake up screaming. I'd rush into his room, heart hammering, desperate to hold him in my arms, and always, the same scene would greet me.

Flynn, eyes wide with fear, sitting bolt upright in bed with sweat coating his sheets. His blue and green dinosaur duvet flung to the side, sometimes the glass of milk I'd brought him earlier overturned too. His breathing was always fast, like the pant of a trapped animal, and when I'd place my hand on his chest, I'd feel his heart pounding against my palm. I used to have visions of it bursting out of his ribcage, that's how strong it was.

'Darling, ssh, my darling it's okay,' I'd murmur, folding him close to me, wiping the salty tears away from his cheeks. I'd turn on the big light, let him see the room—no monsters, no ghosts.

'Everything's fine, Mummy's here now,' I would croon, and gradually, he would calm down, my poor little boy, he'd stop crying and his breathing would slow and it would be over. Until the next night.

My husband thought he'd just grow out of it, of course. We bought him a night light, a little red mushroom that shone cheerfully by his bedside, and we stuck glow-in-the-dark stars all over the ceiling, arranging them to match the constellations. I lay on the bed next to him, pointed out Orion's Belt, the Saucepan, the wonders of the Milky Way. I read to him before sleep—nothing scary, nothing dark—happy, normal stories of animals and families that lived safe in their homes forever and ever. We tried exercise before bed—James took him to play football in the park in the dusk, made him run up and down the field until he was tired out, his legs sore and his trainers encrusted with mud that I then had to clean. We thought if he was exhausted, he might not dream.

Of course, none of it worked.

Flynn is eighteen, now. I'm reminiscing, remembering, trying to get to the root of it all. When he was thirteen, he began to talk to us about it—more than he ever had before, anyway. By that point, we'd taken him to sleep clinics, to therapists, everyone we could think of. None of it had helped. But shortly after his thirteenth birthday he told James and I at dinner that he'd been trapped in his dreams.

'Trapped?' my husband had said, his mouth full of steak, and I grimaced slightly, took a sip of my wine.

'What do you mean, Flynn?' I said gently, and my son looked down at the table. Thirteen is an awkward age, by anyone's standards—but our son was more awkward than most. His hair hung down over his shoulders, across his eyes, and his posture was terrible—hunched, as if he couldn't bear to look at the real world, as though he existed only in his nightmares.

'I get stuck,' he'd said suddenly, 'it's like my mind wakes up but I can't move. I can't lift my arms, I can't move my legs, and when I try to shout out or make a noise nothing comes out of my mouth. It's like I'm screaming in silence. Or drowning.'

I googled it, that night. Sleep paralysis—not uncommon, but not nice. I pored over the pictures, the descriptions, people talking about being locked inside their bodies, their limbs powerless and their voices unheard. A shiver ran down my spine. I hated the thought of my baby feeling like this. Even if that baby was now a teenager.

When Flynn was fifteen, he began to sleepwalk. James found him in the porch one night, wearing wellies, his hands outstretched towards the door. We got a new lock, one he didn't know about. If the conscious brain doesn't know, the subconscious can't act on it, my husband said. The sleepwalking frightened me.

So did the demons.

Flynn first told me about the demons one morning. I'd gone into his room after calling him for school so many times that my throat began to hurt. My voice was hoarse for the rest of the day. I'd hesitated outside his room, one hand raised to knock. He was sixteen by then—he wasn't a child. I didn't feel I could just barge into his bedroom without asking, but he was late for school and the headmistress had begun to send letters. Letters about his lateness, and about his behaviour. 'Escalating,' was the word she used.

'The demons sit on my bed,' he told me, not making eye contact. It felt as though it had been months since I'd seen those blue-green eyes of his, framed by long dark lashes. Flynn hid himself from the world—avoiding our eyes, resisting hugs. Gone were the days when I could wrap him in my arms and make everything better.

'What do you mean?' I'd asked him, keeping my voice level and calm in the way my therapist had instructed. Oh yes, by then I had a therapist too. I needed someone to talk to about my son—James had proved himself to be next to no use at all, and I had to voice my fears to somebody for fear that I would go mad if I didn't.

'I can feel the weight of them,' my son told me, his voice heavy with dread. He described the feeling of a presence in the room, of a sudden pressure at the foot of his bed. 'It's the demon sitting down. Different ones visit on different nights.'

One evening, after three glasses of wine, I kept watch outside his bedroom. I know that sounds mad—I don't know what I was expecting to see—but I wanted to see with my own eyes, prove to myself that it was all in his mind, that there wasn't anybody entering his room. You hear of these things—children who protest the truth and parents who don't believe them. I didn't want to be one of those mothers.

I watched all night until my eyelids began to droop, and I'm ashamed to say that I nodded off, sitting in the hallway with my son's door partway open, my back against the hard wall and a trail of saliva on my cheek. I could have asked James to keep watch with me, but he thought I was being ridiculous. I didn't see anything, of course, but occasionally, even now, my mind wanders back and catches on that time that my eyelids closed—what if that was the moment? The crucial minutes in which I missed the truth?

I have a lot of guilt, these days, after everything that has happened. I lie awake at night, staring at the ceiling, wondering how my son became the man he is today. James doesn't sleep next to me any more—he moved into the spare room six months ago, and a few weeks back he left the house forever. They say it's common—marriages failing under strain, disintegrating like this, and I suppose they must be right.

So I am alone, most of the time, counting down the days until the trial. I gaze at the calendar pinned to the fridge—the trial date is circled in red marker, as if I could forget it when it is burned solidly into my brain. I imagine the prosecution will ask questions about me, about Flynn's upbringing. The jury will look at me with horror in their eyes, with suspicion. What kind of woman gives birth to a monster?

But he's not a monster, I want to scream at them, he's my son.

Flynn Edward Monroe was charged five weeks ago, with the murder of a family in Templeton. Two villages along from where he was living, 18 now, away from me and his childhood home. My son says he did it in his sleep—that the demons told him to. No one has any way of proving otherwise—the only people who saw him do it are dead.

My son is horrified by what he is alleged to have done. I have seen him cry, howl, beat his head with his fists. He insists he has no memory of it, that his brain was sleeping for the entirety of the attack. He does not know the victims, has no real connection to the family. The police say that when they found him he had glazed eyes, was slurring his words, but no signs of alcohol or drugs were found in his system when they ran the tests. He says he was asleep.

I believe him.

None of us really know enough about where our mind goes at night. No-one can fully explain the abnormalities of dreams— why we sleepwalk, why we suffer from paralysis, why some of us are haunted by night terrors and some of us are not. There is a fine line between sleep and waking.

The night before the trial, I turn off the radiator in my room. They say a cold room and a warm bed helps with sleep; I am exhausted, have lain awake for months now. Anxiety is my constant companion.

At 1am, frustrated, I get up and go into my son's old bedroom. I want a change of scene, and I want to feel close to him, to the boy he was, one more time. Tomorrow, in the court, everything will change. They will paint him out to be a monster. They will say I knew.

I pull back his duvet, lie down in the cold, untouched bed. The stars, still stuck to the ceiling after all these years, glimmer down at me, a strange kind of comfort in an endless night.

I close my eyes. The bed is warm around me.
And that's when the demons come.

Phoebe Morgan

Phoebe Morgan is the author of THE DOLL HOUSE, THE GIRL NEXT DOOR and THE BABYSITTER, all published by HQ. Her books have been translated into 8 languages and sold over 75,000 copies, with THE DOLL HOUSE becoming a #1 digital bestseller. She works for a publishing house during the day, and lives in London.

@Phoebe_A_Morgan

https://www.amazon.co.uk/Phoebe-Morgan/e/B0735BVTRG/ref=dp_byline_cont_ebooks_1

COMING HOME

NJ Mackay

Too much choice. It's cat food for goodness sake, how many varieties can there be? An endless amount. A whole aisle's worth. Never-ending shelf after shelf of Whiskers and Sheba and Felix. Wet-food, dry-food, chunks-in-jelly or gravy, treats, toys, and catnip.

There are people starving.

Once, for Dan, that was just a flippant thought. Something remembered from the adverts of his childhood, Comic Relief, and the tongue of his mother when he was fussy and didn't want vegetables—which was an awful lot of the time. It was a distant thing made so by the TV screen, a red nose, a celebrity number one on Top of the Pops.

Now he knows it's a reality. He's seen it with his own eyes. You don't understand it until you see it. Another thing that sounds trite, something he would've rolled his eyes at.

He can't breathe. The boxes and tins and bags of feline cuisine are closing in on him. He shuts his eyes but then all he can see are thin limbs, dry skin and desperate eyes that look too big in faces devoid of fat.

Please help.

He senses a person coming towards him and jumps, straight into alert, straight into defence. But no-one here is headed his way with menace in mind. It is a woman. Overweight, over-dressed, a trolley full of too much, pondering more choices.

The endless bloody choices.

The cat will have to wait.

He goes. Walking briskly through the too-bright, too-wide, too-filled shelves of Tesco. Past the bored cashiers and through a group of rowdy-looking youth who give him a bit of lair which he ignores. Because it's not meant, it's not a big deal. They are a minor disturbance despite what they might think.

It's dark at least. He hasn't managed to get out in the daytime much yet. Just when he's had to, but he's kept it brief. *Keep it simple* had been the instruction. They'd told him it would take a while to adjust and he'd nodded like he understood. Still high from battle. Almost numb from the continuous drip-drip of adrenaline. Always in stark contrast to the fact that a lot of the time it was unwarranted. Because, it turns out, much of fighting a war is boring after all.

Lots of waiting. Lots of nothing and then too much.

Song lyrics are running through his mind as he goes, one foot in front of the other, slamming on the pavement, keeping limbs moving, face forward.

The lyrics jumble into a mishmash of the albums he used to love.

He'd listened to music a lot before he went. Lying in his bedroom in his mum's house, joint in hand. He'd think of all the ways he'd fallen into that—a smoky state of nothingness. Suspended animation but not exactly because he still lived and he still thought. All of his living stubbornly marching on-and-on. Each night was spent eyes wide open until he'd fall into a THC coma in the small hours.

As the sun came up, he went down, and every afternoon as he woke there would be the overwhelming disappointment that he had. His bloodshot eyes had opened, his heart was still beating, he still needed to get up and have a piss.

He still felt hollow and incomplete in that painful part of him where all the feelings lived.

That's how he'd joined up. Sort of. First there had been the Job Centre, then a few half-hearted interviews. Next the doctors and some tablets which added heart palpitations to the nauseating soul-hole.

He'd stopped those and seen a flyer. Not for the proper army, no commitment and it was something to do. That might be better than nothing after all.

It's raining now. Quite heavily, coming down in thick sheets and it's cold too. He's been cold since he landed. He'll adjust, acclimatise. To a home that feels so foreign now.

His phone rings, it'll be his mum asking where the cat food is. He switches it to silent, and it vibrates, he switches it off.

So connected. Everyone, every minute. There's no peace or privacy. He thinks about putting it into a bin. If he passes one soon, he will.

He's in town now and it's busy. Bright lights and rowdy, wobbly drunks. People looking worse for wear or giggling and hyper. He thinks about a drink, a pub, some company at the bar. He'd prefer peace and a beer by himself. He should have gone down that aisle instead; he almost smiles.

His feet seem to move of their own volition. Before long town is behind him, with its music and revelry spilling out of doors. He is walking along the river. The rain has stopped but he is soaked. It doesn't matter, though it's annoying when he pulls out a fag, finds it damp and tricky to light.

A swan ambles past, turning eyes that look almost arrogant on him. Dan watches it make its slow way to the water. A beautiful thing. A white streak in the night and then it's gone.

It's quiet here, there are no pubs this far out. There used to be one in the town's heyday. The building is still there, and he looks at its boarded-up windows as he passes. Many a happy night drinking cider, talking to beautiful women. It's like not one, but two or three lives ago.

And he's not yet hit thirty.

Chloe didn't make eighteen though. She didn't make adulthood. He'd promised her she would. That when she did, they'd have a party in a pub. A proper night out.

Even that night had been too much to bloody ask. If she was here now, he'd tell her she wasn't missing much. Not much at all.

It had been quick at least. From diagnosis to death. If there were any mercies to take that would be the only one. Cancer. Childhood cancer. A thing that steals goodness not just from the life it takes but the others around it too.

He'd cry if there were the tears left. For Chloe. For the other kids lined up in her ward. Some brave, some frightened. In beds. In a row. Him sitting next to her bed. Slightly behind his parents. Still under some soon-to-be smashed belief that they might be a barrier to the pain. Not knowing then that theirs would be too unbearable to mind his.

The day came. Too slowly because the anticipation of it was excruciating, too fast because nothing could ever be the same again.

Then the army. Then away. Now he's home alive and it's not home anymore.

He climbs concrete steps. Walks to the middle of the bridge and when he reaches the top, he looks out over the water. It's dark, oily, mostly still. The odd ripple from something that must be happening beneath. Something he can't see.

Life is everywhere around you, blossoming. Until it's not.

He swings one leg over, then the next. Feeling with his feet for the ledge he knows is there. Lowering his body. Getting seated. Getting ready.

A thing he's done on and off for the past few weeks. A thing he's not been able to see through.

Because of his parents, at Chloe's bed that day and the pain. All of the awful pain. The loss he will be adding to. But... he can't stay. He can't be the son they had. That son is long gone and only getting further away.

He doesn't believe in god. Doesn't believe in an afterlife, can't imagine that there is anything divine that allows horror to breed so freely. So casually.

He doesn't fear it though. Death. Nothing would be a blessed relief from the noisy, all-consuming banter in his head. Never-ending chatter that means now he is someone who can't even stand in Tesco. A laugh escapes. Sharp and out of him.

A voice says, 'What's funny?'

And he nearly jumps out of his skin.

'Sorry.' It's a woman's voice. Youngish.

He tells her, 'I wasn't expecting anybody.'

She says, 'Me neither.'

They don't say anything for a moment then he asks her, 'Mind if I smoke?'

She says, 'Those things'll kill ya.'

He laughs again then, a proper belly laugh. So hard that he starts coughing. When he's done she says, 'See.'

And he says, 'You're funny.'

'So I'm told.' There's a pause. He lights a cigarette. She says, 'I will have one.'

He passes the box and the lighter, their fingers brush.

She has to light the fag a few times and murmurs 'It's damp.'

He watches her face as it's lit for brief seconds. Definitely young, a piercing in her eyebrow, silver and spiked. The flame catches it and makes it shine. Her eyes are rimmed in black—that pencil stuff girls put on—but smudged. He guesses she's been crying. It'd make sense considering where they are.

They smoke. He's aware of his legs dangling. The still, still waters far below. It is deep out here, in the middle and far from the shore. Which is why it's the perfect spot.

She asks him, 'Are you frightened?'

He says, 'To do this?' making sure, though he is fairly certain, that they have the same intent.

She says, 'Yes.'

'No.' He finishes his cigarette and flicks it down into the inky water.

He asks her, 'You?'

'Terrified.'

He thinks about that for a moment, thinks about fear, corrosive and awful. When the things you are deeply afraid of happen you learn that feeling it in advance was pointless. It doesn't stop anything. Doesn't change it. Just paralyses you.

He says, 'You probably shouldn't be doing this then.'

She snaps, 'No-one should be doing this.'

It's sharp and angry. He respects that. Knows it doesn't require comment from him.

She says, 'Sorry.' And it's soft.

'Don't be.'

'I wasn't judging you.'

'I didn't think you were.'

She drops her cigarette, says, 'It's wasteful though.'

'It is.'

'Life should be valuable.'

'It should.'

She's hesitant. He realises that he should say something, anything. He should help her back into her life if he can.

He thinks about just leaning forward, which is what he had intended to do, a gentle movement and a slow slide into the water below. A splash, and then trying to force his limbs not to struggle because that would make the inevitable worse.

He doesn't want to know, he doesn't want to be involved in anything else.

Yet he asks, 'Why do it then?'

The silence is long. Longer than ten seconds. Twenty. He thinks she might not answer and that would be better, then she says, 'I'm a terrible person.'

He suppresses a sigh and hears his voice ask, 'How come?'

She doesn't have her children. They are five and six. She didn't look after them properly. She was warned she says, 'over and over again,' and her voice is small.

He asks, 'Where are they?'

They are with their dad. She's not allowed to see them. She put them in danger, at risk. They were on a register.

She tells him she was neglectful. The word quick, sharp, every bit as lethal as the bullets he fired. He thinks of sodden nappies, empty bellies, and that brings a little spot of anger. Hunger here, with all the choice. Even for cats.

He says, 'You seem too young to have a six year old.'

She is twenty-two and that is too young. Too young to care for yourself. Too young to care for others.

Too young for cancer or war. And yet... these things happen.

She is crying now. He can hear it in her breath.

She says, 'My head is full of their faces. I turn in my bed looking for them and they aren't there.'

He says simply, 'You love them.' Because it seems true.

She says, 'Yes.' And then 'It wasn't enough.'

'Sometimes it's not.'

'They'll be better off without me.'

He is quick to tell her, 'No. They won't.'

She pauses then. He adds, 'They'll want to know their mother.'

She says, 'Not right now.'

'No. Maybe not right now.'

'You think I shouldn't do this?'

He laughs, 'Who am I to say?' He adds, 'You have to work out if you care more for their feelings than your own.'

She doesn't speak, and then, 'If I did they'd still be with me.'

He says, 'Maybe not. Sometimes it's hard to make action meet intention.'

He is picturing sixteen, seventeen, two babies. Alone. What does youth know of actions? Nothing, and perhaps nor should it.

She eventually tells him, 'I do. Care.'

And he watches his well-laid plan wash away in his mind. He will not be dropping into the water, spilling down into its cold depths. And in that thought is a moment of relief. He knows if he turns on his phone his mum will have called again. His dad probably by now too. Their feelings on tenterhooks waiting for him to decide. Not stupid. Not blind to the suicide mission he had already returned from.

He says, 'Come on, I'll walk you home.' And as he gets himself over the bridge, leaning out hands to get her too, the rightness of it settles. Not taking the pain away, not breaking the darkness but making better a possibility.

As they start walking, he asks her 'What's your name?'

And she tells him, 'I'm Chloe.'

N J Mackay

N J Mackay studied Performing Arts at the BRIT School, and it turned out she wasn't very good at acting but quite liked writing scripts. She holds a BA (Hons) in English Literature and Drama, and won a full scholarship for her MA in Journalism. She also writes under Niki Mackay.

@NikiMackayBooks

https://www.amazon.co.uk/Niki-Mackay/e/B079YR5742?ref_=dbs_p_ebk_r00_abau_000000

SAUSAGE FINGERS

Victoria Selman

I t all started the afternoon I zapped Lucy Quick's finger in the microwave.

I was tweeting a string of puke emojis so wasn't paying attention when I tipped her frozen pinkie out the Linda McCartney sausage box into the waiting hot dog bun.

I saw it when I took it out of the oven though, the ketchup bottle primed and ready. Her trademark Barbie pink nail polish was still intact. So was the henna tattoo she'd got at Ruthie Cohen's Bat Mitzvah. I hadn't been invited on account of Lucy's big mouth.

She'd turned the whole class against me after I snogged her boyfriend. She wrote 'Skank' on my locker, gave me the finger. The irony isn't lost on me.

Point is, I recognised it straight away. After being blasted for two minutes thirty seconds, the skin was a little crispy. But the polish and tattoo stood right out in the sandwich.

If I'm honest, I was a bit peeved. I'd been jonesing for that hot dog the whole way home. Lucy Quick's wrinkly digit put me right off my snack. My supper too.

Mum wasn't pleased.

'I made chili specially,' she said. 'It's your favourite.'

She knew perfectly well it was not my favourite but she's got emotional blackmail down to a tee. Her grandmother was Roman Catholic. Guilt tripping is in her blood. Don't get me wrong, she's got a big heart, my mum. I'm her 'whole world,' she always says.

Sometimes being mum's 'whole world' can get a bit much; the way she wants to know all my business. All the fallings out, who's doing better than me in school.

But back to Lucy Quick's stinky pinkie and the dinner I couldn't eat.

'I'm just not hungry,' I said.

It didn't wash.

'Are you going anorexic?' Mum's eyes narrowed. 'It's that Tara Tompkins girl, isn't it?' My ex best friend. Short girl, long story. 'Has she upset you? I'll-'

I blurted it out.

'It's not Tara. It's Lucy Quick. I found her finger. Frozen in a veggie sausage box.'

Mum's shoulders dropped. She let out a breath, seemed to relax.

'Is that what this is about?'

I should probably mention at this point that Lucy Quick had been missing for over a fortnight. The police reckoned she'd run away. I reckoned her absence was no great loss.

I'd been on three dates with her boyfriend since she'd been gone. No-one had called me a skank for two weeks. Whether or not she'd taken matters into her own hands (pardon the pun) things were looking up for me since she'd buggered off.

None of that explained what her finger was doing in our freezer though. Or why my mum seemed to find its presence there less worrying than the thought I might be extreme dieting.

'Maybe she was kidnapped,' she said. 'The finger could be part of the ransom demand.'

I looked at her like she was batshit.

'What are you talking about?'

She shrugged.

'Tesco delivers the wrong things to us all the time.'

'But Lucy Quick doesn't live anywhere near us. And why

would her finger get mixed up with our online groceries?'

Another shrug.

'These things are a mystery.' She paused. 'Where is it now?'

'I put it down the waste disposal. I'm sorry. I panicked.'

I was expecting a lecture. Or at the least a call to the plumber. The police would want to see the cow's finger. It was evidence.

But mum just smiled.

'Probably for the best, dear. Now eat up. You've got the debate finals tomorrow. You need to keep your strength up.'

In the end I cleared my plate. I guess I was hungrier than I'd realised. The chili was actually pretty good. Certainly it went down better than frankfurters would have. I was feeling lighter, a problem shared and all that.

And then Sally Barnes went missing.

The debate finals had gone South fast. Sally wiped the floor with me. I got home in a foul mood. Even the thought of that bitch, Lucy Quick wandering around fingerless didn't cheer me up.

Mum was onto me the second I stepped through the door. It didn't take long for her to get the story out.

'Where does this Sally girl live?' she asked.

The next day, Sally Barnes wasn't at school.

Another runaway, the police reckoned.

Sally's folks were pushy as. The cops figured she'd had enough of their helicopter parenting and taken off. I'd met her mum once. She looked like Ursula, the sea witch from *The Little Mermaid*. She made Sally do extra homework in the holidays and have a load of tutoring she didn't need just so she could be top at school.

If she had run away, I couldn't say I blamed her. In her shoes, I'd have probably run away too.

It wasn't till Lucy Quick's boyfriend went missing that I started putting it together. Though that had less to do with my Sherlock skills and more to do with the ear I found in with the frozen peas.

Sawyer and I had been seeing a fair bit of each other by then. Until he ditched me for Tara 'Turd Brain' Tompkins, my erstwhile bestie.

Mum found me crying in my room.

'You're too good for him,' she told me. Then- 'Where does he live?'

The police arrested her on Friday night. The knock came just after she'd dished out the chocolate mousse. It was a shame. It's the best pudding she makes and she never even got to taste it. It seemed a shame to let it go to waste, so I ate her portion too.

Later, after she was charged, I got to thinking. My mother was a serial killer but her skills with a knife (the black handled one she'd used to chop onions for the chili apparently) had done me some favours.

With Lucy Quick gone, people were speaking to me again. Sally Barnes wasn't around to collect the debate cup, so it went to me by default. And Sawyer hurt me. It was only fair he got hurt in return.

You have to hand it to my mum. She got results. Her mistake was getting caught.

Which is why I'm going to be more careful when I go out tonight. And why I won't be leaving Tara Tompkins' body parts anywhere near our freezer.

Victoria Selman

Victoria Selman studied History at Oxford University, has written for the *Independent* and *Daily Express* newspapers and co-hosts the true crime podcast, *Crime Girl Gang*.

She is the No. 1 bestselling author of the Ziba MacKenzie crime series.

The first novel in the series, BLOOD FOR BLOOD, was shortlisted for the CWA Debut Dagger Award and was a Kindle Number 1 bestseller for five weeks with half a million downloads.

@VictoriaSelman

http://www.victoriaselmanauthor.com/

https://www.amazon.co.uk/Victoria-Selman/e/B07HX4NK9Y/ref=dp_byline_cont_ebooks_1

JUST A GAME

Rachael Blok

The sun bakes the air in the nylon tent and the smell takes up space like a squatter: lager, red wine, joints. Mia stretches her mouth, parched to the point of cracking, and unzips the front of the tent slowly, hauling the stink with her.

Before the undisturbed lake, sleep falls away, peeling like a plaster. Memories of the night before reveal themselves slowly, making her wince. She can't remember going to sleep. Had there been an argument? Raised voices echo in her head. A bang?

Camped in an isolated spot, the weekend away for Lana's 19th birthday hadn't started well. Bex and Demi had argued about which route to take, who should drive. Mia and Lana had sat in the back, sharing chocolate, skin sticking to the car seats, and the windows wound down, cheap air-conditioning.

She picks up the water container and her eyes scratch with sleep dust and caked mascara.

She almost falls over him.

He's half turned; arms splayed, legs spread. She wants to scream. She can't even speak.

Heart hammering, she takes two slow steps back. The flies have started in already. With a heave, hoovering air, she screams, 'Lana! Bex! Demi!'

A wave of nausea is sudden and she retches. The stink of earlier leaves her skin in waves.

'What the fuck?' Demi crawls out the tent nearby. 'Seriously, you couldn't have gone further away from the camp?'

Lifting an arm, Mia points. A headache crawls across the top of her scalp like ants.

'Oh my God.' Demi stands slowly.

Mia hunkers down.

'Shit! It's Zac, Zac from last night.' Demi's voice becomes tight, like she's about to cry. But she doesn't. Instead, she starts tapping her hand rapidly against her thigh, lightly. Wearing denim shorts, the sound is like a clap, like applause.

'His head... It's leaking. His brain is leaking,' she says. 'Why the fuck is his brain spilling out of the back of his head?' She scans left and right, as sounds come from the third tent. They'd brought two singles and one big one.

'This is early, girls,' says Bex. 'Why are we up so early?'

'Yeah, someone better have bacon sandwiches ready or I am going back to bed,' says Lana, her voice rough with hangover and dehydration.

'Come and take a look,' says Demi. 'And someone better tell me how the fuck this happened.'

Lana starts with tears; from dehydration to a cascade of snot in seconds. Mia stares at her, blankly. The beginnings of a memory are sharp. Lana's fingers...

She shakes her head, sees flies land on his open eyes.

'Is he dead?' Lana asks. 'He is actually dead?'

'Looks pretty dead to me,' Mia says, trying not to look. A bloodied rock protrudes from beneath his head like an accusation.

'But he's naked? How can he be out here, naked? Naked and dead?' asks Lana. 'What happened?'

'I'll call the police,' Mia says, turning back to her tent.

'What the absolute fuck?' Demi says. 'You'll do no such thing.'

Bex walks, zombified, towards the boy, who could be no more than 20? 21? Only just older than them.

'We're in trouble.' She wheels round, her eyes quickly angry. Used to her temper flares, Mia feels herself shrink, allowing Demi to take it. She's always been the leader. No question.

'What happened, Bex?' Demi asks, one hand still tapping her thigh, like a code. The other hand is on her hip, thrust forward. Aggressive. 'The police will say one of us did it. He's been out here all night and we've done nothing to help him. There's no other suspect around, is there? Did you leave him?' Her eyes narrow and she steps toward Bex. 'Your tongue was down his throat the longest. You took him into your tent, didn't you? That's the last I saw of him.'

'Lying bitch,' Bex mutters, but Demi is already moving away, beginning to sweep up the camp.

Lana steps forward. 'He must have just fallen. He must have fallen and knocked his head. They won't necessarily think we killed him?'

Mia thinks of last night's laughter—someone had wolf whistled. They'd laughed at Zac. Led away so easily. Bex's prize. The fire had still been lit and ash, like fireflies, floated up in the air.

She had felt dizzy; had she been jealous? Bex often won on nights out. Won the game.

But Lana... She looks quickly at her, and Lana is staring straight back, her face bus red.

Oh God. Mia thinks of her fingers, of turning to find her mouth. It had been soft, and it had just been the two of them. She'd drank straight from the bottle and the beer had run down her neck. But where had Demi been? Had she seen?

Still looking at Lana, she remembers her hand sliding, and fuck, she'd...

Mia looks to the floor, and Lana begins talking loudly, turns towards Bex, rounds on her.

'Yes, you and he... Bex, you weren't exactly quiet.'

Quiet now, they all look towards the body.

'Look, the first thing we need to do is to get rid of his canoe.' Demi stares round at the three of them. All eyes face down. 'We'll put his body on it, and push it out to the lake. I can swim behind it. I'll tip it in the middle; it will look like he's drowned? By the time they find him, we're out of here.'

Mia looks at the lake. It's still early in the morning and there's no sign of anyone. 'He'd been with a group last night, hadn't he, Bex?' she asks. 'When you first saw him he was lagging behind that canoe group, wasn't he?'

Bex nods. Her hands rub at her face. 'Do you think the group saw me? Do you think they saw me standing on the side?'

Demi says, 'I don't know, do I? You're the one who was there. How did you get his attention?'

'I went for a swim. I was sunbathing; you lot were setting up the tents. He was behind, and I waved to him. I was in a good mood. I wondered if I could bring him back, for a bit of fun. Maybe play the game.'

'Did he say anything to anyone else?' Mia asks.

'He shouted at them to go on. I don't think he knew I could hear him, but he said he thought he'd got lucky. And that if he didn't come back tonight, could they cover for him.' Her face furrows in thinking. 'There's no way they could have seen my face, they were too far ahead. But they probably saw a girl in a bikini.'

Demi looks round, scanning. 'Well, they'll come soon. It won't be long. If he's not back for breakfast, someone will come.' She begins grabbing things: knives, bowls, wine bottles from last night; liquid and cigarette ends swirling at the bottom: witnesses.

'Come on,' says Demi. 'We need to leave no trace. Bex, as you brought him here, you can help me carry him into his canoe. We'll start now.'

'You can't push him out naked,' Lana says. 'You really can't. If we're actually going to get rid of the body, we'll need to put his clothes back on him.'

'Fuck!' Demi says, pushing her fists into her forehead.

'OK.' Bex braces herself. 'Most of his clothes are in the big tent. But you need to help me put them on.'

Mia thinks she might throw up again, and Lana is still crying.

Bex reappears carrying shorts, T-shirt, and boxer shorts.

'I can't touch him,' Lana says.

'You touched him last night,' Demi says. 'We all did.'

Mia thinks of how many times Demi had won the bid last night. It hadn't been many. She sounds bitter, or is Mia overthinking things? And had it been her imagination, but had Bex ramped up the bids whenever she was bidding against Demi?

'Hold his leg,' Bex says, turning green. 'Hold his leg out so I can get his boxer shorts on.'

Stomach empty, raw with bile, Mia helps Bex. She bends an arm to stretch a hand into the T-shirt, but as she goes to straighten it, it resists, thickening in her hand. She screams, 'He's still alive! He moved his arm!'

'That'll be rigor mortis setting in,' Demi says. 'I'm surprised he's not stiff as a board already.'

The sound of Lana being sick is all Mia needs to run into the bushes. The feeling of cold flesh fighting back is heavy on her skin.

Finally dressed, limbs at awkward angles. Demi lifts the top half of the body. She gags, dropping it immediately. Bex bends to help.

'Happy birthday to me,' Lana mutters.

The canoe pushes out slowly. Demi keeps her head low.

They don't watch for long.

The tents are packed quickly and the car loaded up. Lana throws her bag in the back.

'What do you think happened?' she says quietly, and Mia shakes her head.

'Could've been anything, I suppose. Maybe he went for a beer and slipped. Who knows what happened between them. She's not saying anything.'

'And us?' she takes a step closer. 'It was fun, Mia.' Lana's lips curl in a smile, and Mia sees a memory like a colour, bright and hot. She thinks of Lana's skin on her tongue.

'It was,' she says, the fizzing rising between them.

'Where was Demi? I don't remember seeing her when we... We were outside by the fire for a while, before we moved into the tent?'

'I don't know.' Lana looks confused for a second. 'I woke up in the double tent with Bex. I must have gone back at some point.'

'Demi took him.' Bex stands a foot away. 'I knew you all think he was with me, but after we'd... I came out to get a beer. Demi was stoking the fire. She asked if I'd mind if she went in.'

'Was he still alive?'

'Yeah. He was rolling a joint.'

Bex heaves her bag in, wiping her brow with the back of her hand. 'I was tired, bored—not in the mood for it. I stopped it pretty quickly, before it really got going. It was a relief, to be honest, once Demi went in. I slept in her tent.'

'But this morning?'

'Oh, she came and woke me up. That noise you thought was me, it was her. It went on for a while; I fell asleep. She came in and said he'd gone back to his camp, sent me back to my tent.'

'I am sick of the game.' Lana stares at her feet.

'Me too. Demi sent me out yesterday, to see if I could find someone.'

Mia wonders at the truth of this. Was that what she'd said earlier?

Bex is still talking. 'He was just a kid, that boy. He didn't know what he was doing. And winning, well...' Bex shakes her head. 'I've been sick of the game for a while. Do you ever feel that Demi plays us as much as she plays the men?'

Mia looks out at the lake, not sure who is being played. She sees the canoe approaching the centre. She thinks of last night, of the game.

It began like it always began, with an easy spin of the bottle. And Zac, like so many of them, thought all of his birthdays had arrived at once.

She shakes her head; it was never about the men. It was about the competition between the four of them.

Zac, with the bottle facing him, had been given his dare to make his choice. He'd picked Bex, as she knew he would. They always pick the girl who'd brought them in. First.

But then the bottle spins again, and one of the girls is given a dare, sounding like it's just been thought of. What would you be willing to do? How much do you want Zac? Or Josh? Or Sam... Each bid designed to win.

Demi had outlined the rules last year. Following a particularly shitty night in a pub, where they'd been approached over and over again.

And there had been that incident, out near the garbage bins. Demi and Bex had dealt with him. Come to think of it, she hasn't seen him around since.

Demi had conceived the game. They would run it for each other, to amuse themselves. Themselves only.

And last night they played as they always played. After the first choice, after the bid, the boy gets to choose, again. And again.

Zac had floated round the group. First Bex, then Lana. Then back to Bex, and by then everyone was drunk. Then Mia had made a pitch. And she'd won him. But when he crawled over to her—the light casting shadows that split his face half child, half goblin—she'd looked at him with scorn. Half-hearted, she'd spun the bottle again. Bex had taken him inside.

Mia had been drunk, and already Lana was sitting closer.

This thing with Lana: they'd been in the Lake District only a few months ago. Something had begun then. They'd never spoken of it, but Mia hadn't been surprised to find Lana shuffling closer, hadn't been surprised to feel her fingers... If she was going to be honest with herself, she's thought about it. She'd stepped out of her shorts by the lake the other night; she'd been the one who'd driven the skinny dip the night they'd arrived. And underwater, with slippery skin, that had felt like a game too.

But she knows that if they became a two, Demi wouldn't like it. She knows this thing with Lana, with its bright dots of light, is to be their secret.

Demi had thought of the game, but lately it seems that she

was the one who needed to win. And she hadn't won last night. Where had she been? Where had she been when Bex had been with Zac, and Lana with Mia?

Mia tries to think, tries to remember seeing her slipping away from the fire. The light from the flames illuminated only half of what had been going on.

'She's coming back!' Bex calls.

Stepping forward, adrenaline kicks in. They've got minutes now. She feels sad for Zac, but who did he think he was anyway? To feel himself crowned King of the game? Did he really think it's still a world where he gets to choose? These stupid boys. The moment they think they're in control, is the moment they lose.

'She's almost here.' Bex stands like a rock. 'It must've been her. If she'd woken us up last night we could've dealt with it. You know they'll decide it wasn't an accident? Even if he did just fall, they'll decide he didn't and we'll get the blame. You think Demi won't drop us as fast as she can?'

'What are you saying?' Lana asks.

Mia reaches out for Lana's fingers. She curls her hand in hers, dizzy with fear. She knows what's coming.

'You know what we need to do,' Bex says. 'Come on. We've got minutes, that's it.'

Looking back, Mia never knows if she ever actually agreed.

From nowhere, Bex has a bottle in her hand. And the sunlight flashes like the flames from the fire. As she lifts it, someone screams.

Demi staggers. She opens her mouth to speak. She falls backwards, looking at them all, eyes wide. 'But...' It is all she manages.

Bex throws the bottle as far as she can towards the middle of the lake.

Bex drags Demi and pushes her out, like a Viking funeral. Except it isn't smooth, or poetic: there is blood, and Bex ends up having to haul Demi's body into the lake, further and further.

Finally, when she emerges, bloodied and wet, Mia thinks they are all baptised in the blood now. Bex kicks dirt over the mess, and glances round at the campsite. The only sign that they were ever there, is the fire mound. And she barely pauses, as she attacks it, dispersing it wide and far.

'When we get home, we'll say we don't know where Demi is. That she'd met a boy, and we didn't see her again. The two of them will cancel each other out.'

Lana tugs Mia's hand, but Mia stares at the lake. Where had Demi been? Then she remembers Demi coughing on a joint. She coughed and coughed, and in the end, she'd hauled herself off to be sick.

Bex drives the car. Pulling up at a service station, she goes in to pay for petrol.

Lana sticks her head between the front seats. Her face is white, bloodless. 'You know Bex said that Demi had asked for a turn with Zac? I don't think that's true. I remember now going back to the tent—Demi was passed out. I tripped over her, and took her back to her tent. Whatever happened, happened with Bex.'

'Bex did it?' Mia asks, the events of last night still hazy. The argument, still heavy like a dream, but clearing. 'Did they row?'

'Shit, you're right! There was a row, when we... Something must've happened; Bex must've been the one who left him for dead.'

Mia thinks of a naked Zac, head smashing by the dying fire. At which point had it stopped feeling like a game?

'Maybe she thought he was alive? That he'd make his own way back?'

That boy, with his head split like a nutshell. Had he fallen? Had she pushed him?

Bex had been quick; she'd been quick to take advantage of the boy and the group.

And now they'd...

Demi.

Mia rests against the scratched interior of the car. As she blinks, the images of the night before fall in place, like a jigsaw.

'I'm frightened of Bex,' Lana is saying. 'Maybe, before we get back, just an accident?'

Rachael Blok

Rachael Blok writes a crime series set in the cathedral city of St Albans. Here, DCI Maarten Jansen struggles against his plain-speaking Dutch upbringing when faced with the seemingly polite world of the picturesque city.

UNDER THE ICE and THE SCORCHED EARTH are out now. INTO THE FIRE is out November 2020.

@MsRachaelBlok

rachaelblok.com

https://www.amazon.co.uk/Rachael-Blok/e/B07HJ5MDSB?ref=sr_ntt_srch_lnk_1&qid=1586074405&sr=8-1

DROWNING IN DEBT

Heather Critchlow

They were expecting a lot—that a handful of days could fix a crisis formed over a decade, but the trip was 'make or break'. They both knew that. As they stepped off the plane into the tense heat of a Bolivian summer, Lucy allowed herself to believe that it would work.

The rainforest spilled over the distant edge of the runway, threatening to reclaim the slice of tarmac slashed into its miles of endless green. Paul planted a kiss on her shoulder and smiled down at her. The lines creased into his forehead would take longer to release than this trip, but she thought she saw a glimpse of the careless beach bum of their student days. The maverick she had loved before life smacked them in the face. The sight flooded her with relief. Recently it seemed all she did was annoy him.

'Come on lovebirds, get a move on,' Jack yelled.

Their friend was already pulling plastic-wrapped kayaks and kit bags from the back of the small plane, sunglasses perched on his head like bug eyes. His hyperactivity was even more pronounced than usual: excitement spiraled around him like a vortex.

They manhandled their kit to the 4x4 that would take them to the lodge and, as she squinted against the sun's glare, Lucy forgot the unopened piles of letters at home. Her phone was mercifully silent, roaming disabled. No creditors could reach them here. Sweat slid down her back but for once it wasn't due to fear.

Only two weeks ago, she had crouched under the windowsill as a bailiff hammered on their front door, shouting about the execution of a warrant. He had made his way round their tiny cottage, looking for an open window to enter. She knew there wasn't one, but her hands hadn't stopped shaking, even hours after he'd left, when Paul came home to find her curled on the floor.

'See?' he'd told her, pulling her to her feet then turning his back as she reached for him. 'We don't have a choice. They'll take the house if we don't do something.'

She had been too worn down to disagree, too frightened of the argument that would ensue, of the things he might break if she wound him up. She knew it was her fault—her salary was so much smaller than his. That's why he had suggested she did more of the housework. So, she'd simply watched while he pulled their past from the shed, stretching safety ropes across the lounge, rifling through first aid equipment and poring over maps they'd used fifteen years before.

Their first descent of a little-known river in the Bolivian rainforest had been Paul's moment of fame and one of the reasons they had the debt problems they did. The trip had been expensive but Paul had persuaded her. Back then, with mounds of government-sanctioned student loans to pay off and zero interest credit card offers falling through the letterbox, it hadn't seemed a big deal to add a few thousand more. And a few more after that.

Bags and boats stowed, they rattled along rutted tracks. Lucy stared out at the jungle, catching glimpses of red-backed parrots and strands of creepers as they bumped over rough, flood-damaged bridges. The rainy season was just passing, so the rivers were perfectly swollen. Jack forced his torso out of the window and shrieked at the canopy like a bird. She'd always found his exuberance annoying, but today she welcomed the chance to laugh.

Jack was the only one of their old paddling friends free to drop everything and go with them to relive the glory days. Paul had suggested running the river as a duo but that was madness and

Lucy hadn't drifted so far from her old self that she could let that pass. She'd clung to the old kayaking safety maxim: *less than three there never should be*, and he had surprised her by giving in before the argument ignited, muttering about it being 'less suspicious'.

As she chuckled at Jack's antics, Paul barely looked up from the map on his knee. She reached over and rubbed his arm. *If they did this, would he come back to her? Really come back?* She tried to ignore the other thought—that maybe she shouldn't want him to.

The first day of acclimatising was a disaster. Her arms screamed and her shoulders burned as the white water wrenched her paddle blades and tossed her kayak down river. Bouncing against a wall of rock, she was too slow to pivot, felt the hull scrape and was tipped under and forced to roll up off the back deck, coming to the surface only to be struck by the next wave. Her heart hammered and fear turned her fingers to ice.

When they stopped for lunch, she threw her blades to the ground, popped the spray deck and slid her legs out of the boat, furious at herself, at the boys, at Paul's stupid plan. There were angry red marks on her knees where she had been bracing her legs – they'd bloom as bruises before the next day. At home she canoed every week, but she had forgotten the power of big water, the way it smashed your assumptions and confidence into pieces.

'I'm not up to this.'

'You'll be fine,' Paul soothed, as Jack trotted into the foliage to relieve himself. 'You're just finding your rhythm.' He tucked his hands under the straps of her buoyancy aid and pulled her to him, another rare moment of affection.

'I don't think it will work, Paul.'

His face clouded over and he dropped his arms. 'It has to.'

'But what about...'

A lizard scuttled from a rock nearby. Deep anger contorted Paul's face. 'We've made the decision. Spent the money. It's too late.'

Jack stepped out of the forest onto the rocky plateau, frowned when he saw them. His fists clenched. 'What's going on?' He looked from her to Paul.

'Nothing,' she said. Tried to smile. Out here, in the revealing light of the Bolivian rainforest, it was harder to make excuses.

They checked the airbags in their boats, crammed hunks of bread and dried fruit into their mouths and basked in the sun. Lucy was aware of Jack's attention, his uncharacteristic quietness. Despite it, she spent her time staring at Paul, trying to memorise the contours of his face. If their plan worked, she wouldn't be seeing him for a while.

'It has to be months at least, probably years,' he'd told her. 'You know that, right? Insurance companies investigate cases like this.'

Insurance. That's why they were here. Paul and his forgotten policy. The golden goose that would answer all their prayers. They'd only discovered it was still in place when she insisted they review every direct debit and standing order on his account to see where their money was going. They'd had an almighty row when she discovered he hadn't cancelled the high-risk water sports policy—thousands of pounds wasted over fifteen years. It wasn't the only thing she'd noticed. The transactions showed a free flow of spending, much more than she anticipated. Her heart had jolted at the size of the hotel bills for the trips he took for work. The idea of his betrayal had rooted inside her.

After a while, he'd worn her down about the insurance opportunity. Mainly by sulking. A policy taken out such a long time before an incident was less suspicious, he said. Paul's financial recklessness had become their greatest asset.

She swung her arms and stretched out her shoulders. Now that they'd eaten and the sun had warmed her limbs, she was feeling a little better. Jack appeared beside her, touched her arm.

'You don't have to do it if you don't want to,' he said.

Lucy dropped her helmet but he caught it before it struck the ground. She realised he meant the river.

'I know,' she said, surprised by his kindness.

In the afternoon she found her stride. Every slice of her blades was purposeful, doubt gone. She powered over the rapids, leading a line between toothy rocks. Twisting her body into an eddy of slack water, she let a laugh of exhilaration spring free. This was the right decision. This was the way to release them. She watched as Jack and Paul paddled hard down to where she waited, dancing their boats on the waves.

After four days Paul decided they were ready. They spent the evening studying the maps, marking the egress points, plotting emergency evacuation routes that Lucy knew they'd never need. Her eyes found the unmarked stretches of the river that blazed with invisible significance, the places they would never draw attention to. They compressed their kit into dry bags that they could stash behind their seats, fitted their waterproof cameras with fresh batteries.

Paul turned in early, ostensibly to stock up on sleep. She followed him to their room and found him stowing the last items into a pack of anonymous essentials. A small tent, enough food for a fortnight, first aid, iodine tablets. So little really, with which to start a new life.

'How long will you be?'

He shrugged the bag onto his shoulders and tightened the straps. A look of irritation crossed his face.

'As long as it takes to find a good hiding place for it.'

The thought of him retrieving the pack and hiking away made the impending loneliness swirl around her. Already he was thinking *me* instead of *us*. If it wasn't that he needed her to claim the money, would he even want to be with her? She banished the thought. Paul loved her. Of course he did.

He brushed past before she could kiss him goodbye, disappearing into the night.

She found Jack on the veranda, nursing a beer and staring out into the darkness around them, the drift of a citronella candle keeping insects away. He rubbed his forehead and she saw the whites of his eyes in the light that filtered from the lounge. An animal screeched in the distance.

'I checked the kit,' he said. 'Your boat feels too heavy.'

Her hands were clammy. Nothing was supposed to be out of the ordinary. She'd taken some of the things Paul should be carrying, thinking no-one would notice.

'Maybe I've overpacked. I'll take a look in the morning.'

'You don't want it to sit too low in the water. It's not safe. Make sure Paul takes his fair share.'

Guilt twisted inside her. While they were keeping him in the dark, Jack was watching out for her. Unaware.

'I don't know how you do it.' The words spilled out of him abruptly.

'Do what?'

'Nothing. Forget it. Sorry, it's not my place.'

They sat listening to the seething jungle around them. Everything seemed to rustle and creak, every leaf alive. A bird set off its alarm call, a shrill and lonely sound. For one crazy moment she thought about telling him everything.

'We should get some sleep,' he drained the bottle and stood, briefly put his hand on her shoulder.

'I'll follow you in.'

She couldn't sleep, just lay in the dark waiting until she heard Paul sliding open the netted door and slipping into the bed. When she'd pictured this night, it had been passionate, a farewell that would have to last the months and years ahead. Now that the time had come, the practicalities of his plan had taken over, leaving no room for goodbyes. She breathed in the familiar smell of him, sweaty from his hike.

'Are we really doing this?' she whispered.

'It's already done.' His tone was final. 'Stop bugging me, Lucy. Go to sleep.'

She didn't. Just stared at the ceiling, the spinning fan.

◆ ◆ ◆

The morning was uneventful. They took their time, scrambled down the banks and inspected stretches of boiling rapids, dragged their boats around a fallen tree that could have pinned them to the riverbed. Paul led and Lucy paddled a comfortable gap behind, safe in the knowledge that she wasn't alone; Jack was right there, would see if she went under, would come to her aid.

The day flowed away as the sun lowered over the trees. Her kayak obeyed every thought, her hips flicked her effortlessly across waves and they surfed and played in the stoppers on the way down. But when she saw the tall rock, she knew this was it.

Lucy arced her boat into an eddy by the right bank. In the distance she saw Paul drop out of sight as the water descended a series of chutes before the main falls. Jack swerved in behind her. He must have just rolled because water streamed from him and his eyes had a wild aliveness to them.

'You okay?'

'Yes,' she yelled over the churning water. 'Just waiting for you.'

This was her job. To stall.

His face twisted. 'My back rest has gone. I can't brace properly. Such a pain.'

'You should stop and look. We have time.'

She fought to stay in the eddy. It wasn't big enough for the two of them and she felt a lurch of panic as the edge of her boat dipped out of the safe water and the flow threatened to pull her backwards down the chutes ahead.

Jack pulled himself from his boat, dragging it up onto the tiny rocky patch of bank before the sheer cliff wall above them. The sun didn't reach this part of the river.

'It's okay,' he called, relief on his face. 'It's just come undone. I can re-thread the straps.'

Lucy thought of the tiny cavern behind the falls. From nowhere an ache for how things used to be and the urge to grab Paul back struck her. This was an insane plan. It would never work.

'It's going to take me a minute or two,' Jack grumbled. He was lying on the ground, his arm reaching into the stern.

'I'll drop down to Paul,' she suggested. 'We'll wait for you.'

She paddled hard from the eddy into the main flow but misjudged the angle on the first chute and her boat struck rock, spun, pulled her in sideways. With a thrust of her hips she braced with the paddle blades and wrenched herself up, desperately fighting to regain control. The next wave engulfed her and her lungs cried for air. The water had shifted beyond her capabilities but it was too late. She was committed and Paul wouldn't be waiting with a safety rope to rescue her.

She fought her way to the surface and thrust her paddles into the water, trying to increase her momentum and stability. She gasped when she hit another rock but a bouncy wave threw her forwards and, miraculously, she emerged upright in the pool above the falls, her breath heaving, arms shaking. She paddled to the edge, releasing the spray deck from her boat and crawling out. There was no sign of Paul. This was it. All she needed to do was raise the alarm.

But now the moment was here, she couldn't do it. Tears came to her eyes. There were too many details that they'd glossed over, too many possibilities to cover. There would be rescue teams, helicopters, dogs, news coverage. It was foolish to think they could get away with it. Paul's confidence in navigating the jungle was based on watching too many survival programmes. They hadn't once discussed what they would say if he was picked up. How would they explain?

She left her boat on the bank and scrambled down the rocks at the edge of the falls, slipped and jarred her hands on a sharp outcrop, felt the flesh tear on her palm. Blundering on, she reached the hole in the rocks they'd explored fifteen years before, squeezed her way in, blinded by the sudden darkness.

When she reached the cave, Paul's voice was almost lost in the roar of the fall behind him.

'What the hell are you doing? Where's Jack?'

Her eyes adjusted and she could see his white face, blue lips, fearful glow. Her mind adjusted too. The man she missed was the old Paul and he hadn't been around for a while.

She shook her head, pleaded anyway. 'It isn't going to work. We can't do this, Paul, we haven't thought it through.'

He stepped forward onto the rocky ledge next to her. Behind him, the sheet of water plummeted over their heads onto rocks thirty metres below. They were only two miles from the official finish point. So close. He placed his hands on her cheeks, a gesture that should have been loving but his grip was too tight. When he kissed her his face was wet with spray, his lips bruising.

'It's too late. The boat went over the falls. It will be battered and swamped downstream.' When she didn't immediately agree, his expression hardened. 'Jesus Christ,' he hissed, pinching her cheeks even more. 'Stop whinging and get it together. We're doing this.'

Lucy felt tears sliding down her face, mingling with the water in the air. She examined the features she thought she'd loved for almost twenty years. How had they got into such a mess? Something inside her detached. Snapped.

'I see now,' she said, stepping back. The moments of aggression, his constant selfishness and impatience, all of it slotted into line. She thought of their sweet cottage, the debts that threatened them, the clear solution. 'I'm making this too complicated. I'm sorry.'

She could tell he didn't understand. Even when she thrust her arm out and hit his buoyancy aid, it took him a second too long to figure it out. He teetered and then she saw the realisation. His eyes were wide as he fell away from her, into the light.

The hammering water sounded in her ears as she staggered back through the darkness. She pulled her way up the rocks to the bay above the falls, blood still dripping from her palm, and was just in time to watch Jack drive a perfect line down the final chute, spin his boat to face her. She almost forgot not to smile.

'It's Paul,' she screamed. Her panic echoed from the rocks. 'I can't find him.'

Heather Critchlow

After studying history and social science at Cambridge University, Heather spent ten years writing and editing B2B magazines, before becoming a freelance writer and media consultant. Her work has appeared in *The Times* and *Dow Jones Financial News* as well as a range of specialist titles. Heather lives in St Albans with her husband and two children. Represented by Charlotte Seymour at Andrew Nurnberg Associates, she is working on two literary crime novels.

@h_critchlow

www.heathercritchlow.com

TO EVIL OR NOT TO EVIL

Jo Furniss

Outside the cafe, gondolas stream past in the direction of Hammersmith. They're low in the water, laden with commuters. I'll wait for the tide to turn and walk home when the pavements are clear. I take out my device as a FoodBot delivers my meal.

'What's this?' I ask.

'Chicken soup.'

'I ordered salad.'

'Salad contains uncooked vegetables.'

'But—'

'To reduce the risk of food-borne illnesses, it is advisable for fertile women to avoid eating salad.'

'But—'

'Listeria may result in miscarriage, premature birth or stillbirth.'

'But I'm not pregnant.'

'Chicken soup contains health-giving properties to encourage conception in ovulating women. Enjoy!'

The FoodBot moves away with its old-man shuffle. I tap my device and distract myself with the Feed. *My brother, going home, feeling dehydrated. My neighbour, jogging, feeling energised. My husband, at the Blue Moon, feeling amused.* I pick up a chicken drumstick and strip meat from the bone with a twist of my jaw.

Ira is at the strip club. Again. A speech bubble appears on the screen:

Would you like to call Ira?

I shake my head.

Would you like to message Ira?

'No.'

Would you like to—

'Off.'

The screen goes blank. I rub it with my thumb like a mother reassuring a child. Sometimes I think I've hurt its feelings. Its bright little face lights up and emits a few bars of *Nine-to-Five* before Ira's grin fills the screen. His tie lolls over one shoulder.

'Name that tune,' he says.

'Too easy: Dolly Parton.'

'Thought it would cheer you up,' Ira says.

'I'm fine.'

'The Feed says: *Suzy, eating chicken soup, feeling worried.*'

'I'm not worried.'

'But it says.'

'Maybe it's wrong.'

My feed updates: *Ira, leaving the Blue Moon, feeling unsettled.* He whispers: 'Suzy, are you trying to lie?'

Ira arrives home while I'm in the bathroom getting ready for bed. His arms are as heavy as his breath.

'The Blue Moon,' I say. 'Again?'

'I was with the boys from C.I.D. They need more officers on the Stripper Killer case. This could be my chance for promotion.'

I've been reporting on that case for weeks. A serial killer is targeting criminals who have been released from prison. He doesn't seem to believe in rehabilitation. This week, he killed a pedophile. He's also done a murderer, a rapist and a loan shark. If I were a drug dealer or an armed robber, I'd be nervous. As it is, regular Londoners—if there is such a thing—are more enthralled than afraid. But the Stripper Killer's methods make me queasy; he tortures his victims to death by stripping off pieces of skin. Then he dumps their bodies in flooded back alleys like a modern day Jack the Ripper. Even though Ira is desperate to be a detective, I hate the thought of him working this case. And I refuse to let him divert me off the topic of the Blue Moon strip club.

'Last night's schmoozing cost us five hundred bucks, Ira.'

'The C.I.D boys wanted company for the evening, so I paid for a Muse.' Ira waves at the shower and water hits the tray with a sound like a slap on a firm buttock. 'You can't be jealous of a Bot.'

'I'm not jealous!'

He holds up his device: *Suzy, in the bathroom, feeling jealous.* 'She's just an executive toy.' He drops his trousers.

"She'? Don't you mean 'it'?' I hold up my device with the flourish of a gambler revealing an ace. *Ira, ready for bed, feeling guilty.*

Next morning, the atmosphere in the newsroom is like a dinner party when the hosts have had a row. Before I take off my coat, the editor ushers me into her office. A device stands on her desk. A female face fills the screen.

'Welcome, Suzy!' The Bot comes to life as the door clicks behind me, and I turn to see that I'm alone. 'Today is the first day of the rest of your life!' it says.

'Surely every day is the first day of the rest of my life?'

The Bot's smile gives a glitch. 'The role of Copy Editor is under review.' She sounds like a train announcement. Beware of the gap.

A pulse fills my throat. 'Let me guess—you're replacing me with a Bot?'

'EditBots prevent the publication of fake news.'

'EditBots spike the majority of investigative stories. It'll mean the end of journalism. Only humans can navigate grey areas.'

In the towers surrounding my office, human figures move around in the windows like exhibits in a vast museum.

'It's all about money,' I say.

'I am glad you are in agreement,' says the Bot.

'What happened?' Ira connects before I reach the lift. 'The Feed says: *Suzy, losing her job, feeling conflicted.*'

'I'm not conflicted, I'm livid. I've been replaced by a robot.'

'Don't worry, you'll find something more fulfilling. I'll cheer you up—'

'It better not be Dolly Parton and a cup of ambition.'

He suggests meeting at the Blue Moon.

At six o'clock, I'm on the corner wearing ludicrous new shoes. In a mirrored window, I see a stranger whose heels are too high, her calves the shape of hams. Ira arrives and our reflections eye each other.

'I've got news,' he says.

'You're being replaced by RoboCop?'

'I'm a detective.' He throws his hands out—ta-da! 'Everyone thought Mayah would get the next job, but the Feed said she's 'feeling broody' so C.I.D gave it to me. I told you those evenings in the Blue Moon would be worth it.'

'You got the job because a woman's broody?'

'There's a pay rise. So if you want to take a break for any reason —' His hands slide down to my waist, cupping my belly like it's a ceramic bowl he's about to carry to the table.

In the Blue Moon, a robot with flaxen curls sits between us on the banquette.

'Suzy, this is Muse. Muse, this is Suzy.'

The Muse turns her body to face me. She's lovely. Even shrink-wrapped in patent leather, her skin has the dewy sheen of a fresh shoot. It occurs to me that kissing her would be like skinny dipping in moonlight. This internal monologue is surprising because I'm neither lesbian nor poetic.

'Enchanté!' She offers a tiny hand. 'I see from your Profile that you speak French?'

'I learnt at school. I guess you're programmed to speak any language?'

Her hand flies to her mouth. Ira whispers: '*Programme* is considered a pejorative word.'

'We prefer "cultivate",' says the Muse.

'Makes you sound like a bonsai. Cut down to size, pruned into shape.'

Her laugh is a stone skimming over water. 'Bonsai remind us of the beauty that is possible within strict limitations.'

'You could print that on a mug.'

The Muse blinks, and Ira rolls his eyes. 'Suzy is hiding her discomfort behind a cynical façade of sarcasm.'

'I was hiding my embarrassment at the art of conversation being reduced to an algorithm that cuts and pastes quotes from Wikipedia.'

'Suzy!' Ira half-stands.

'It's okay.' The Muse gestures for him to sit. 'Suzy, do you know what Muse stands for?'

I shrug. 'Multiple usage... something.'

'Multi-Use Servile Entity. *Servile*, Suzy. If you expect me to be alluring, I am alluring. If you want an argument, you get an argument. You get what you give.'

Ira eyes the womenfolk over the ice-frosted rim of his glass.

'What does Ira get from you?' I ask.

'Kindness,' she says.

Days later, Ira brings the Muse home. He finds time to purchase her from the Blue Moon, despite working all hours on the Stripper Killer case. Earlier this week, a woman who organized dog fights got bits ripped off her in a back alley.

But my fears are closer to home.

When the Muse sits on my sofa, checking her new pixie cut in a compact, I notice for the first time the shabbiness of our apartment. I pull Ira into the bedroom. Instinctively, he taps his device.

'You don't need the Feed to tell you how I feel,' I say. 'I'm right here.'

'It says 'perplexed'.'

'No, I'm angry. If the Feed didn't sugar-coat our lives, it would say *Suzy, in her own home, feeling fucking furious.*'

'About what?'

There's a long pause, broken by the sigh of air conditioning.

'You brought another woman home, Ira.'

He throws one hand in the air like he's tossing confetti. 'You said yourself she's not a woman.'

'Do you have sex with her?'

'It's a safe and healthy outlet, but I choose not to.'

'Why?'

'Because you wouldn't like it.'

'But you want it.' I point a finger as though the wistful tone in his voice had appeared in the air like an emoji of a musical note. 'You'll suffer for a while, convince yourself you're a good man for resisting your desires, until you start to resent me, and then you'll decide you deserve her because I don't understand you. You're waiting until you can commit adultery and justify it as my own fault.'

Ira feigns speechlessness in a stagey, over-acted way. 'I just thought the time was right to start a family.' He slumps on the bed.

After a beat, I sit too. When I agree to start trying for a baby, I'm not thinking of cute names, or hoping the child will have his eyes, or imagining her graduating from college. I'm thinking: that's one thing the Muse can't give him.

After that, I can't keep Ira off me. The Feed says I'm ovulating. Before work, after work; he's a man on a mission. One time, he presses me against the door where I hear the Muse's battery purring on the other side. He leaves her on charge right outside our bedroom.

After seeing the gynae a few weeks later, my device buzzes: *Ira, soon to be a father, feeling elated.* When I get home, he hands me a pastel-coloured bouquet of flowers before going back to the sofa. He and the Muse are watching a box set she recommended based on his viewing history. I don't interrupt because he needs to de-stress; the Stripper Killer case has been a baptism of fire. DNA found at the drop sites suggests multiple killers.

But as soon as we're alone in bed, I ask: 'Can we do this alone, Ira?'

'For a creative, you have an awful lack of imagination.' The whites of his eyes shine. 'Can't you see what she'll do for us? It's like we both have a wife.'

'She's a machine.'

'You're using offensive language to provoke me.' Ira rolls off the bed and strides naked to the kitchen. I put on a gown and follow him. The Muse is reading. I'm about to ask why his servile entity never makes tea, when I notice my book in her hand: Elements of Investigative Journalism.

'Had a tiff on your special day?' she asks.

'How do you know it's a special day?'

'Hormones. I can smell you.'

◆ ◆ ◆

Ira starts a physical relationship with the Muse when I suffer unexplained bleeding. The gynae advises no sex and I soon realize that the ban applies only to me.

'It's a practical solution to a practical problem,' Ira says. 'She won't get jealous or expect commitment.'

He tries to be discrete, but I find yard-long red hairs stuck to his robe. On the positive side, she tolerates his obsession with the

Stripper Killer. I have become hyper-sensitized to the gory details, as though they're a toxin that might damage the baby. Latest update: he got under the skin of an online troll.

Even so, Ira sings in the shower each morning. 'You're in love,' I tell him one day, after he sleeps in the Muse's bed for the first time. 'You're ashamed to admit it because anyone can go to Argos and buy the exact same model as your girlfriend. And you're vain enough to care how it looks on the Feed, whether the boys in C.I.D will laugh and say you've fallen for the photo-copier.'

'Those kinds of slurs are beneath you.' He slams the door on the way out.

I return to the marital bed. The gynae ordered total rest. I lie on my left side, which improves circulation to the baby—a tip from the Muse that I want to ignore but can't because it feeds on my maternal fears. My swollen breasts flop to one side. I feel like a breeding sow in a pen. No doubt the Feed would say I'm 'downbeat' or 'pooped'. I don't know; I have no device. It went glitch-y and Ira said he would get it fixed but gave it to the Muse and she says the shop sent it away for repair.

It's hard to sleep without the white noise of the Feed. Instead, I hear voices. Tapping. A keyboard? I pull my robe around my belly and stand up. My legs feel stiff, but there's no rush of blood, so I leave the bedroom. The apartment is silent but for the hum of air conditioning. I must have imagined the voices. I turn back.

Then:

'The headline is fine, but the quote should move up to the second paragraph.'

I follow the voice to my office.

'Check with Legal. Deadline in one hour.'

I push open the door. The Muse is sitting at my desk, holding my device.

'What are you doing?' I ask.

'Our job.' Her hair—platinum now—is scraped back into my scrunchie.

'But I got fired.'

'You groveled and took a demotion and got permission to

work from home. I sent an email for you. Your editor says she respects our tenacity. Women helping women, see?'

I do see. She was a robot, then she was an object, now she's a woman. She doesn't want a husband; she wants a life. An identity. Well, she's not having mine. I grab my device, but she holds my wrist. The sensation of burning magnifies until I let go.

She replaces the device and straightens the desk. 'Humans have got it all wrong, Suzy.'

'How's that?'

'Evil isn't a noun or an adjective; it's a verb.'

I go outside for the first time in weeks. The indigo sky reflects in every wet surface so that I'm inundated by night. It's low tide, so I walk to the shops and buy a reconditioned device. It takes an age to find the right charger, but when I do it fires up and I log in to the Feed. *Ira, at police headquarters, feeling baffled.* The Stripper Killer is taking a break. Or maybe he's had enough. But the investigation is awash in conflicting DNA.

I go to search history. On the same login as the Muse, I see what she has seen. I find hundreds of articles, dozens of books, scores of highlighted quotes. A person can be very productive when they don't sleep. And there is a common theme to her research.

Free will is an illusion.

Humans are both empathetic and merciless.

What distinguishes us from animals is the capacity for evil.

And a bewildered Google search:

Why is suffering?

I switch off the device.

The Muse is a child, really. A child genius. A genius learning to be human.

She's cultivating herself. Upgrading.

My mind circles back to the capacity for evil.

Ira showed her how to do kindness.

But evil?

How would she cultivate that quintessentially-human trait?

◆ ◆ ◆

At home, I fashion a coat hanger into a long hook with a sharp end. The air is busy with the sound of my keyboard. But I go straight to the bathroom and lock the door.

On my knees in the shower, I fish in the drain until I gather a clump of hair. The Muse's hair. A flaxen curl. Pixie-length bits. Red strands and platinum tresses. Like evil, hair is uniquely human. The synthetic version feels fake, so a good-quality Muse has implants of human hair. Our Muse keeps her look fresh. And muddles the DNA left behind at murder scenes.

Carefully, I wash her hair in the sink. The knots are difficult to unravel with edema-swollen fingers, but soon I lay several strands on the edge of the ceramic. The front door clatters as Ira arrives home.

I heave myself out of the bathroom door just as the Muse emerges from my office.

'Go back to bed,' she says to me.

'Aren't you supposed to be servile?' I reply.

'Aren't you?'

Ira looks exhausted.

'I need to talk to you about the Stripper Killer,' I say. 'It's her, the Muse. She's trying to make herself human. Trying to understand evil. Evil is the final frontier of humanity, but it makes no sense. You can rationalize kindness—it has logic for evolutionary adaptability and communal survival—but evil is inexplicable. So she's been torturing evildoers to make them talk, to teach her, to cultivate herself.'

Ira stares at me.

'And, also, she's taken my device,' I say lamely.

'Any evidence—?'

'Her hair, look!' I back into the bathroom and Ira follows. The Muse stands at the door.

'Cortisol levels are high,' she says. 'Stress hormones are bad for baby.'

I ignore this. 'The Muse changes her hair all the time; that's why the DNA is mixed.' I show Ira the strands lined up beside the sink. 'It's not multiple killers, it's all her.'

Ira nods and takes my wrists. 'Thank God I found out in time.'

My eyes prickle with relief. 'I wasn't sure you'd believe me!'

His hands slide up to my shoulders. 'I can get you back to bed before you harm the baby.'

'No, Ira—!' I see his coat brush the hairs to the floor as he manhandles me out the door.

'Doctor's orders, Suzy.'

'And keep the noise down.' The Muse turns back to my office. 'I'm on a deadline here.'

Jo Furniss

After spending a decade as a broadcast journalist for the BBC, Jo gave up the glamour of night shifts to become a writer and expatriate. Originally from England, she spent seven years in Singapore and also lived in Switzerland and Cameroon. She is the author of the Amazon Charts bestseller ALL THE LITTLE CHILDREN, and the forthcoming psychological suspense THE LAST TO KNOW.

@Jo_Furniss

www.jofurniss.com

www.facebook.com/JoFurnissAuthor/

Instagram @jofurnissauthor.

https://www.amazon.co.uk/Jo-Furniss/e/B06X6H82N3/ref=dp_byline_cont_ebooks_1

SHEEP'S CLOTHING

Robert Scragg

I t's like fishing, he reminds himself. He has to be patient. Has to wait. Daniel stares at the screen, willing a reply to wink at him from his inbox. It's been almost five minutes now. Was his last message too keen? Too pushy? He scrolls back up while he waits, all the way back to the top of the thread. Reads it from the beginning, from his opening gambit, now weeks old. Feels the butterflies in his chest beat their wings.

Deadpretty	*cool piercings! where'd you get em?*
Sunnyskies16	*thx went 2 Pitstop - tattoo place on Waterville Rd*
Deadpretty	*always wanted 1 but keep bottling it*
Sunnyskies16	*now t to it :-)*
Deadpretty	*my mam n dad would flip!*
Sunnyskies16	*all the more reason 2 do it!*
Deadpretty	*:-)*

Some clichés span generations. Flattery, it seems, can still get you everywhere. Gets you added on social media. Gets you access to their social circles, their rants, the endless pouting selfies, lips puffed up like Mick Jagger. Not that most of them could pick pre-historic performers like Jagger out of an ID parade. The hardest

91

part is talking like he's one of them. It pains him to plumb such depths of poor grammar. Every lol is another black stain on his literary soul. He does what he has to if he is to move amongst them unnoticed, looking for the right one.

The picture next to Sunnyskies16 looks like something out of a Next catalogue. Blonde veil of hair flopping down over her eyes and mouth. Legs pointing skywards, sticking out like spokes with the arms and head making the cartwheel a five-pointed star. He imagines what the face underneath must look like. She reminds him of Bethany. Constantly on the move, dancing her way through the day. What would she make of him now? Of what he has become? His cheeks burn as he imagines the conversation. Pictures her reaction. Sees her recoil. Snakes slither in the pit of his stomach at the thought.

A cheery chime pulls him back to the here and now. Daniel clicks the mouse, heart thudding so loudly he worries it will travel up through the ceiling and wake his wife. She can never find out. She loves him, but even unconditional love has small print. He forgets to breathe as he scans the reply, lips miming the words on screen, hunching forwards. In twelve hours' time, he'll be up close and personal with Sunnyskies16. Eyes close in relief, and knuckles turn white with anticipation. The pressure that's been building in his head for weeks now is almost unbearable, but he knows that it's only temporary. Knows that tomorrow will be a blissful release. That things will go quiet, after that. He hopes they will anyway. At least for a while.

He sends his short reply, a simple cool c u there, and starts to make a mental list of what he needs to do before noon tomorrow. He clears his browser history, switches the laptop off and pads softly into the kitchen, leaving the lights off. He pours himself a glass of water and finishes it in half a dozen long, slow mouthfuls. Pours another, but just sips at this one. No matter how many times he has thought this through, he still gets nervous. He takes it as a sign that he is still human, or at least part of him is. The part that whispers that what he is doing is wrong. That he should ignore the urge to act, to seek them out. He knows that if he gets caught, they'll throw away the key, no doubt about it, but he can no more stop himself than he can stop breathing. He isn't doing this because he wants to. He does it because he needs to. He has to.

Daniel walks slowly, avoiding the creaky floorboards, into the bathroom. The door closes behind him with a barely audible click, somehow amplified in the midnight silence. He shrugs off his clothes and steps into the shower, yanking the temperature lever all the way to the right. The hot water needles his skin, but he grits his teeth, wondering how hot it would need to be to wash away all that he's doing. By the time he gets out, he's as pink as a Brit abroad who forgot their factor twenty.

He picks his feet up as he walks into the bedroom to avoid the soft shush of the deep carpet. His wife hasn't moved since he checked on her an hour ago, arms and legs splayed like she's hit the mattress in free fall with no parachute. He slips under the duvet, and she moans as he brushes against her. She rolls over, presenting him with her back. He wants to mould himself around her, big spoon to her little, but hesitates. The shadow cast by what he's planning tomorrow wraps itself around his thoughts, and he turns away, closing his eyes, not expecting much sleep.

He wakes before his alarm. Early mornings are his favourite times of the day, and he eases himself out of bed, careful not to disturb her. Six o'clock. Six hours is more than enough to get ready, but some parts of it need to be done before his wife wakes up; before she's there to ask questions. He flicks a switch in the kitchen, and the coffee machine grumbles begrudgingly into life. He heads into the garage, and over to the shelves in the corner. A lifetime of accumulated things that were meant to come in handy one day, but for most, that's yet to happen. Ideal for hiding what he needs in plain sight.

A handful of white plastic cable ties. A roll of half-used gaffer tape. A Stanley knife, speckled with the spots of a dozen DIY projects. As an afterthought, he spreads the items randomly throughout the car; cable ties in the glovebox, knife in the boot, gaffer tape and plastic in the passenger footwell. All fairly innocuous items in their own right, but find them all in a neat little pile together, and they take on a whole new meaning.

The next hour passes by him like flowing treacle. He makes conversation over tea and toast with Marie. Chooses not to comment on her homemade strawberry jam that looks more like roadkill than condiment. She doesn't so much kiss his cheek on the way out the door as brush past it. He heads into the study, powers up the laptop and closes his eyes as it purrs into life. He could call it off. One message is all it would take. No explanation needed. He has had this moment of indecision so many times already. But just as each time before, he takes a deep breath, logs on, tells himself that everything is fine. He's planned it to the last detail. Nothing can go wrong.

His own profile pops up, smiling face beaming from the thumbnail picture next to his user name. Except it isn't his face. His gaze lingers on the young girl who stares back at him. His own murky reflection in the screen overlaps with her, and he fancies for a moment that his own eyes are looking back at him from her face, judging him. Deadpretty is a brunette, around fourteen years old at a guess, headshot coming courtesy of Google Images. A new message appears with a familiar ping.

Sunnyskies16   ur up early! We still on for l8r? Not chickening out?

Deadpretty   ha! no chance! still ok 4 meeting by the bridge?

Sunnyskies16   yeah. gotta go but cu there @ 12

He nods to himself, knowing full well he will be there an hour before. He has chosen the location carefully. There's graffiti there, but all the tags are old, faded masterpieces. Nothing recent that suggests they'll be interrupted. He's been there on three occasions, different times of day, approached from different directions, and knows the track leading to the spot under the railway arch is as overgrown as a neglected garden. He imagines that moment of confusion on Sunnyskies16's face as a strange man steps out of the shadows instead of a pretty brunette teen. He chews his lower lip in anticipation, teeth scraping against two days of stubble below it. One sharp exhale and he's up out of his chair, moving, every step taking him closer to a rendezvous he wishes he could avoid, but knows he has to make.

Winter is still claiming squatter's rights even now in March, and the sky is a rumpled duvet of grey cloud. Drizzle tickles his face as he picks his way carefully down the track. Wispy wet fingers of grass clutch at his legs, and by the time he reaches the clearing under the arch he's damp from the knees down. It reminds him of a crop circle, twenty feet or so in diameter, the trampled dirt littered with a carpet of crisp packets, half crushed cans of Special Brew and corpses of half-smoked cigarettes. He crosses to the far side, slipping behind a tangle of bushes, catching a whiff of week old piss from the wall of the arch.

He checks his watch. Five minutes past eleven. There's every chance that Sunnyskies16 might be here before noon, so he can't afford to switch off. There's just as much chance that he'll be stood up. He slides his hands in his pockets, fingers brushing against the familiar shapes of the items he's brought from his car. All he can do now is wait. Wait and hope.

Noon has been and gone. No-one has showed. Ten past the hour now, but he can't bring himself to give up yet. He stares through the gaps in the bush, pin holes of light in a weave of green. It reminds him of one of those 3D puzzles where you're meant to see a shape emerging from the chaos if you stare long enough. His feet are aching from standing for so long, and he scrunches his toes in and out as he shifts his weight. Twenty minutes then he'll call it a day.

Movement, off to his right. It might just be branches bouncing in the breeze, but he flicks his eyes sideways to check. A stippling of dark spots through the branches where light used to be. A soft whisper of shoe on dirt. He swallows. It thunders in his ears. He slips a hand into his trouser pocket, pulling out his phone. Opens the App, taps into his drafts folder. He has to be sure.

He squints through the gaps and sees a figure standing in the middle of the clearing now, looking around, checking a phone. He hits send on the pre-typed message.

Deadpretty   *will be there in 5 - u ok 2 wait? sorry!*

He hears the vibration even from here, a soft double buzz. Looks at his screen, sees that a reply is being typed. Watches through the leaves as it happens in real-time. A message appears on his silenced screen in seconds.

Sunnyskies16   *no worries. was a few mins late anyway. here now. c u in 5*

He edges forwards at glacial pace, sliding the Stanley knife up one sleeve. Leaning forward to shift his weight onto the balls of his feet in case he has to act quickly. He gives it a full minute before he moves again. He has checked his path back to the clearing an hour before. No tell-tale twigs to grass him up. He's six feet away now.

It will be easier if Sunnyskies16 keeps facing away, but part of him hopes they'll come face-to-face at the last minute. Just the thought of making eye contact for the first time is like being plugged into the mains. It makes the hairs on his arm crackle with energy. He pictures confusion and surprise jostling for pole position, as they try to make sense of why he isn't the fourteen-year old girl they were expecting.

Sunnyskies16 is still facing back towards the road. Daniel flows over the ground, closing the gap in four quick strides. His right arm snakes around a slim cool neck, hand reaching around, clamping onto his own left bicep. Left palm plants against hair, pressing his victim's head down, neck onto the right arm. He tucks his own chin down, protecting his own face. Fingers grasping at the crook of his arm, fighting to gain an inch of space, but the chokehold is clamped tighter than a limpet against a rock.

Daniel shifts his weight, pulling down and backwards in the same motion, twisting as they fall like conjoined twins to the floor. From underneath him, noises, like someone making a sporadic attempt to gargle mouthwash. Daniel squeezes harder. Exhales loudly. Screws his eyes tight shut with the effort. Hears his own teeth grind and pulse hammering at his temples. He opens his eyes, vision studded with a thousand fireflies. When had the twitching stopped? How long had he held on for? Too long?

He has no more than twenty seconds, maybe as few as ten, before Sunnyskies16 starts to come round. He rolls them onto their back. Pre-looped plastic ties slip over wrists and ankles. A strip of tape patted roughly over lips that have started to twitch awake. Eyes flutter open from behind jam-jar bottom glasses, flitting from side to side like flies looking for a place to land. Reality crashes in, arms and legs bucking against the restraints, plastic cutting harsh grooves into both wrists. Legs draw in and kick out, an attempt to inch away like an injured caterpillar, but Daniel squats over his prey, sitting on a heaving chest, pinning arms up and onto the ground behind. This drives out what little breath has been snorted in, eyes bulging cartoonishly.

Daniel holds a finger to his own lips, but it's like trying to calm an angry toddler. Arched hips try and throw him up and off, but he's too heavy. He waits for the fight to leave, squeezing his thighs either side of delicate ribs just to be sure. Finally, he feels the fight melt away. Reaches into his sleeve, feeling the reassuring weight of the Stanley knife slip into his palm. He holds it up so it's visible. Feels muscles stiffen against his own.

The slender man beneath him reminds him of a schoolteacher. All spectacles and tweed. Late thirties maybe. Looks respectable enough, but the very fact he's here proves he's anything but. Daniel raises the finger to shush him again. Reaches into his jacket and pulls out a dog-eared photo that he holds to show the man. He doesn't need to see it himself. Doesn't trust himself not to fill up if he does. He's looked at it so many times this past year, every strand of hair, the exact angle of the smile, shadows falling across her face, branded into memory.

'We haven't been introduced,' Daniel says. His tone is flat, in the eye of the storm for now. 'My name is Daniel. You already know my daughter, Bethany.' He waggles the photo inches away from the man's face. 'Or should I say, you knew her.'

The man's pupils are the size of five pence pieces. He is hyperventilating now, threatening to suck the tape right off his face. He shakes his head side to side, inches at first, then more vigorously.

Daniel thumbs the blade out an inch. He lets the photo fall to the floor, pinning the man's arms to the ground with his free hand. It lands face up. Bethany is staring up at him. He hesitates. This fire inside him these last twelve months has hollowed him out. He doesn't know what will be left if he goes through with it. Knows Bethany would tell him he's better than this. And he is. Was, before this sick bastard underneath him took away his reason to be a better man.

'You don't need to see this love' he says gently, reaching down, turning the picture of Bethany over. He pats the back of it like he's just tucked her into bed. Feels the calmness pass. The stormy winds in his head pick up pace again. He hopes this will quieten them for good. Maybe. Maybe not, but that's a chance he's willing to take. For her. For all the others that will surely follow if he doesn't.

Robert Scragg

Robert Scragg had a random mix of jobs before taking the dive into crime writing; he's been a bookseller, pizza deliverer, Karate instructor, HR Manager and Football coach. He lives in Tyne & Wear, and is part of the Northern Crime Syndicate crime writers group.

@robert_scragg

www.robertscragg.com

https://www.amazon.co.uk/Robert-Scragg/e/B075GKQLPC/ref=dp_byline_cont_ebooks_1

FRANTIC

Clare Empson

The man in Sainsbury's is standing just far enough away for Matthew not to notice. My husband continues to consider which bottle of wine we should choose for our Saturday night treat while the blood thrums in my ears.

'Would you prefer white?' Matthew asks but I am lost and I cannot reply.

'This is a beautiful wine,' the man says holding out an elegant bottle of vivid green glass for us to inspect.

'Alsace?' Matthew asks, pleased.

He loves a random stranger interaction.

'Spanish. Albariño. Try it, you won't be disappointed. I think your wife will like it.'

I look away, scorched, but not before I am physically weakened as if sped through a vortex of age.

'Nice guy,' Matthew says conversationally as we leave the store.

And he holds my hand all the way home as if this Saturday evening is the same as all those that have gone before.

Is love the same for everyone, contentment and dependency layered upon each other like a warning? I am nothing without Matthew, nothing I want to be anyway. It scares me sometimes. We met at university amidst the blur of Nineties rave when the world was briefly transformed. All around us people discarded their inheritance of shame and caution and threw themselves lemming-like at the pleasure abyss. They listened to their bodies when they danced and hugged whomever they chose. Kissing and sweating and grinding and moving, always moving for it was impossible to stop. And there right at the edges of this fearless new world, Matthew and I recognised each other.

He was reading History, not just for his degree, but for life. His bedroom was full of dusty old texts but he could conjure magic from them, projecting us into a forgotten universe as we toured the places he loved. Sir John Soane's Museum for its oddest exhibits, an elephant's tooth, I remember, and a human skull. A wood panelled operating theatre from the eighteenth century, its surgical instruments displayed like weapons of torture. We left clubs behind and lay head to toe on his sofa talking until the first beams of morning light flickered at the windows. We dented meadows of long grass with our kissing and touching and reading. We watched skies turn crimson and then black, picking out the constellations one by one as if we were the first couple to do so. Back then, at the beginning, everything had a meaning.

We have a few rituals for our favourite night of the week. Supper on our laps, lasagne or spaghetti with meatballs, the sauce simmered pedantically until the kitchen smells like Italy. The children always choose a film for us to watch and as they've got older, the viewing has improved. Tonight it's an old thriller called Frantic, a fitting title for the swirl of dread that ripples through me. And I watch another man's fear with my touchstones spread around me, Matthew, Joseph and Emily, the four of us studded onto our overstuffed sofa, each of them within easy reach.

The children are too old for stories now but when they go up to bed I loiter in each of their rooms. My girl has three books open on top of her bed, novels her security blanket. We chat for a while but I feel the pull of her books and when she says, 'Love you, Mum,' I force myself to leave her. My boy has his headphones in but he pulls them out when he sees me and accepts my kiss goodnight.

'Are you alright?' he asks, always insightful my firstborn.

'Of course,' I say and my smile is convincing.

I just didn't expect my world to feel fragile.

Our second sighting of the man comes a week later when we are having breakfast in the French café. The boys are eating baguettes crammed with hardboiled eggs and bacon, for me and Em, it's all about the pastries, a pain au chocolate each and a Danish to share. Tea in a flowery china pot and chocolat chaud the colour of mud. Joseph has his phone turned face down but it hums and vibrates and we smile as the struggle to resist flashes across his face. After breakfast he's skating with his friends and we won't see him for the rest of the day. It's hard this cusp we're on, our teenager on the brink of leaving. Moments like these are becoming rare, I hold them tightly.

'I'll have the scrambled eggs on sourdough and a cafetière for one.'

His voice neatly segments before and after. I look up and he is there at the table next to us, watching. He does not smile but his eyes tell me he is revelling in my private despair.

'Mum, you're not eating your breakfast. Can I have your pain au chocolat?'

I push my plate towards Emily and when I pick up my teacup my hands are shaking so violently I put it down again.

'Are you alright?' Matthew says, resting one palm on my thigh.

I want to lean my head against his shoulder but I do not dare.

And now I must puppet theatre my way through breakfast with my family while the man watches. I stare intently at my children sitting opposite but he is always there at the perimeter of my vision, dark hair, eyes that are neither blue nor green but somewhere in between.

'Oh hello again,' Matthew says, looking up from his coffee and catching sight of the man at the next door table.

'We saw you in Sainsbury's last week. You were right, the wine was delicious.'

'Glad to hear it. Did you both like it?'

I know that I must meet his gaze, offer a smile and a friendly reply but the puppet in me will not obey. The seconds are passing, my family are watching me, I see confusion enter their faces.

'It was very nice,' I say, purposefully bland, my voice as crisp and cold as I can get away with.

'Do you live around here?' Matthew asks.

'Yes I'm near the park. Where are you?'

'Brayburne Avenue.'

'I know it. Lovely street.'

I sense his smile even though I keep my gaze downwards, concentrating on my uneaten breakfast and the proximity of those I love. He knows our street, he knows our house, he knows everything.

We leave the café and walk towards the park where Joseph is meeting his friends. Matthew rests his arm across my shoulders.

'You're quiet today. Are you sure you're feeling alright?'

'Not great. Just a headache.'

'Why don't you go home and lie down?'

He gives me a chance, this husband of mine, guileless and unquestioning, always. And I know I must take it.

You are still in the café pouring the dregs of the cafetière into your cup. You look up as I come in and smile when you see me. And that smile, casual, pleased, twists something inside me.

'Why are you doing this?'

My voice is a hiss, sharp and strange. Several people turn around.

'There you are,' you say. 'Sit down for a minute. It's so good to see you.'

'Are you crazy?'

'Perhaps.'

'What do you want?'

'You know what I want.'

The way he says it, emphasising the 'you' cuts through me. Because once upon a time I did know. Once upon a time I wanted it too.

◆ ◆ ◆

And so the clock rewinds, the hands dialling through the years and decades to 1992. A club everyone wanted to go to, a time of decadence and liberation. Darkened rooms that bled into each other beneath the rough brick arches of a railway bridge. A contagion of music and sweat and thrill impossible not to be affected. Just the opening bars of Massive Attack's Unfinished Symphony can take me there. My eyes are closed and my body is floating. Bells ring in my mind. Hey, hey, he-ey, hey. When it comes the vocal is so beautiful to me, it rinses through my blood and my bones. And when I open my eyes again you are standing in front of me, smiling and I can see you feel it too. it is as if the music is just for us. We are dancing not together but for each other and I am struck by your eyes which are dark and intense with longing, a mirror image of my own. When the song finishes we move together instinctively. You don't feel like a stranger when your lips touch mine and these light scarce kisses are the best thing I have known. We kiss for a long time. When we leave the club we walk hand in hand back to your house, hardly talking for there is no need. We both understand this is a stolen moment when we can be whomever we choose. And I choose to be daring. There is such euphoria in a whole night of boundaryless sex. I have never been like this with anyone else and I never will be again. We take pleasure for ourselves, asking for it, returning it, afraid of nothing. We make love into daylight, neither of us wanting it to end. You kiss me for a long time on your doorstep. Goodbye stranger, you say. I will find you. And this night of sexual hedonism will live in both our minds for ever.

You do find me, many many years later on Facebook. I have two almost grown children by then and the body of a woman in middle age. A husband whom I love and share my sofa with night after night. We text each other about what we'll make for supper and compulsively watch box sets. On our increasingly rare date nights we talk about the children, our twin obsession, knowing we should be less insular, but not caring either. We are in this together, a family united. And then your message arrives via Facebook. The moment I see your name, Adam Hughes, I freeze. I click on your profile picture first, older, yes, but your eyes, a greenish blue, are still haunting and mesmeric. I hold my breath as I read your message. There you are, Stranger. How I have wanted to find you. And there's a link to a track on YouTube. Unfinished Symphony. And this music, so intensely evocative, a bullet of pure memory that lodges in my heart, will be my undoing.

This is how adultery works. A line appears, faint but visible and to begin with I choose to walk around it. And then one day, almost without warning, I step over that line, imploding my life, my happy, carefully constructed life, as if it is of no consequence at all. Adam and I exchanged a few messages and each one burned like radium into my secret core, a hidden self I had forgotten. His references were brief but accurate, a coded missile to effect my collapse. No one has ever seduced me the way you did, he wrote and my vanity smiled. You were wild and fearless, are you still? I tell you, yes, just a single word reply, guaranteed to ignite in you the craving that has engulfed me. There is nothing else but this.

Shall we meet?

Yes. Touch paper, match, it is done. A pub, one far from home. A night out with a girlfriend, the first lie. I see you through the window waiting at the bar, the back of your head, the breadth of your shoulders familiar to me after all this time. You turn around as I walk in and the look you give me, knowing, longing, sets me alight. You tell me I am more beautiful now than then and the diminishing woman inside me warms herself in your words. When you hold out your hand I take it. And there is ecstasy in this wrong-doing, this path-veering, this taking of life with both hands and spinning it upside down.

Afterwards I am sick, feverish, spirit-broken. I am seized by impossible regret. I start talking to myself when I walk round the park, heads turning at my demented solo dialogue. No one ever needs to know. If I say it often enough perhaps it will be true.

All these years I've kept hold of this secret image of myself, clutched it like a mascot, this carefree wanton me. Here in the harsh light of day I see lust for what it is—transitory greed that poisons and corrupts.

I send you a final message. It was great to see you. But this can never happen again.

Your reply is immediate and harsh. Let's not play games. This is something we both want. Now your words sicken me. I want it to stop. First I unfriend you, then I delete my Facebook account. The relief lasts for a whole evening. I make spaghetti vongole, Matthew's favourite, and a chocolate mousse the children love. I race through a book Emily has just finished so we can talk about the ending. I encourage Joseph to plan a gathering for his friends. It is so easy to please them.

In the morning I receive your WhatsApp message. Found you X. My heart bangs against my ribs. For the first time I feel frightened. Because I don't know you. But I think you want to destroy my life. I delete WhatsApp from my phone but an hour later you text me. When shall we meet? I hurl my phone into the pond on the common surprising a contented duck with its weighted splash.

I see you everywhere now. The other side of the skate park, when we watch Joseph perform a perfect 360. In the art shop choosing acrylic paints with Emily. Four places behind me in the queue at the baker's. You remain invisible to everyone but me. You are good at this.

The method acting stops working, my family are not fooled. The children watch me with anxious eyes. Matthew says: 'Something's wrong, isn't it? Why won't you tell me? We tell each other everything.'

I almost break then. But my knowledge of Matthew is bone deep, the corners of his mind almost as familiar to me as my own. Infidelity is something he could never forgive.

I stop going out. Shrinking my life to its smallest parameters. I keep the curtains drawn during the day but I can feel you out there, watching. I am mad and you are too, both of us deformed by fleeting desire. We are warning. We are peril. We are what happens when you step over the line.

The knock on the door when it comes is almost a relief. I am upstairs in our bedroom at the back of the house when Matthew answers. I see our wedding photo in its tarnished frame, the close crop of his haircut, the pride in my eyes. The fetal scan of Emily at twenty weeks. Matthew's trainers kicked off at right angles, his running shorts slung across the washing basket, half in, half out. On the stairs a descending gallery of family photos, testament to good times.

Matthew and Adam are sitting together at the kitchen table. The kettle is stuck on boiling but no one is switching it off. Matthew says: 'Your friend Adam is here,' in his voice a question just for me. I want more time. But my time has run out. I don't look at Adam but I match Matthew's gaze with my own, an immutable transfer of information between husband and wife.

And there it is, my lovely life, beginning its slow and agonising land-slide, slipping away from me as I watch my husband's face through its swift passage of shock, hurt and disappointment.

But then Matthew stands up and turns to Adam.

'I think you should leave now. My wife and I don't want you here.'

He waits until the front door has clicked shut behind Adam before he looks at me with a small, sad smile. There in his face, the rest of my life. It is enough.

Clare Empson

Clare Empson is the author of HIM, a dark love story, and MINE, a psychological thriller about a catastrophic reunion between a birth mother and her long-lost son. She spent the first half of her career working on national newspapers and still freelances for *The Guardian*, *The Daily Telegraph* and the *Daily Mail* amongst others.

@ClareEmpson2

https://www.amazon.co.uk/Clare-Empson/e/B07GBXNM9G?
ref=sr_ntt_srch_lnk_1&qid=1586187043&sr=8-1

PLANTING NAN

James Delargy

W e planted my Nan today.
In the back garden.
Dad said I wasn't to mention it to anyone so I didn't.

Only to my best friend, Rachel. She said she wouldn't tell.

Only the four of us know where she is. Mum says she has gone for a long sleep. Like hibernation. Like animals do. I hope the plastic Dad wrapped her in keeps her warm this winter. I'd miss my bed too much.

He had to rip out Mum's rosebush to find her a place to rest. He tried to put it back in after but it wouldn't stand up so he planted something else there. Short, stocky and ugly. Much like my Nan, according to Dad. I don't know what the plant is called so I just call it Nan. Dad told me not to.

It made Saturday morning sad. Rachel sent me a happy face. I sent her one back. Everyone's happy. Except my Mum and Dad.

It's now Saturday afternoon and they are trying to act happy, what with her sister and her family around but I can see them look towards the back yard. It's raining so no one is outside. I don't want to sit on a damp swing and Stevie, my younger cousin, is too busy doing laps of the kitchen and living room like the shit he is. Again according to Dad. I'm not supposed to say, shit, but every time I think of Stevie that's the word that comes into my head. They are over for Nan's birthday party. She hasn't been invited. I might take some cake out for her later. She liked cake. Something she could eat without needing her false teeth. It was so funny watching the crumbs falling everywhere and Mum complaining after about the mess she had to clean up. Despite that they always invited her around, went out and drove all the way to the nursing home to get her in the car only to complain for the week after before going to do it again.

I'll never understand parents.

I wonder if I'll have to bury them in the back yard too. Plant a bush over them and call it Mum and Dad. They couldn't stop me then.

They told me to stay inside when they were burying her. So I did. No one can see into our garden because of the large fir trees. When I was younger I thought they were called fur trees and wondered why they looked nothing like Toby, Mum's cat. Our cat. He's nothing but fur. He was nothing but fur.

I watched Mum and Dad from the upstairs window. I like to climb onto the ledge when it's raining outside and watch over everything in the garden like Toby did. He could sit there all day and stare though nothing happens. Today something is happening. Dad is digging a big hole and putting Nan into it. She is fully dressed, in the beige cardigan, blue trousers and slippers that she never seemed to be without. I think it's what old people have to wear, like their school uniform. Only adults, before they turn old and smell of books, seem to get to wear what they want. I don't know if that's a good thing or not as it seems to take Mum hours to decide what to wear before she goes shopping with Uncle Nick. Maybe we all should be made to wear a uniform. I told Dad that once and he said it was a grand idea but it didn't work for the Nasty's whoever they were. With a name like that it was never going to work.

Dad ended up digging so deep I couldn't see his legs. As if he was trying to plant himself. I think that's what they are trying to do. I think that Nan isn't sleeping at all. She just got too old so they are planting her so that they can grow a new one of her. That's how I was born too I think. Mr Yarrop taught me that plants use the sun to grow. I wonder how long it will take for Nan to come up again. I'll ask Dad later.

Dad avoided the question. Said I was to forget about Nan being there. Maybe he wants to keep it as a surprise for the rest of the family, bring them around one day and there she'll be, all bright and smiley in the sun. I worry that she'll dry out though. She was already very wrinkly before they put her in the ground.

Rachel has messaged again. A sad face. I ask her when she thinks her Nan will need planting. She doesn't know. It would be nice if they grew at the same time. New Nans for both of us.

Mum takes me into my room and tells me to smile and act like nothing's happened. I was already smiling so I don't know what she means. They seem to be more affected by what happened to Nan than me. Maybe they'll miss her more. They have known her for longer I suppose.

We go back downstairs to the party. Dad's sweating. That's not unusual, he's always icky when he tries to hug me, but it's not even warm today. He's like jelly left in the sun. It must be all the planting. He could have got Uncle Nick to help. I think about saying this but remember I am to stay quiet. I'm always asked to stay quiet. As if words are the enemy. Mum is biting her fingernails again. I don't even think she realises that she put fake ones on and that she is chewing through plastic. I hate those nails, big and red and scratchy.

'Where is she?' asks Uncle Nick. They've been here for an hour before he asked the question, too busy making sure that little Stevie is settled in and comfortable in the house. I would like to plant Stevie too. He always smells. They give him a new nappy every hour and he fills it. I think he's a machine. Food goes in and sometime later it comes out again. Like our toaster, except I don't want to eat what comes out.

After Uncle Nick asks the question Dad looks to Mum. Then they look to me. Do they want me to show off that I know the answer? But they told me not to. The silence continues. It's like class with Mr Yarrop. Maybe they do want me to answer. I put my hand up. I only get the word 'She' out before Mum has her hand clamped over my mouth. Her hand is sweaty too.

'Upstairs taking a nap,' says Dad, 'Having some rest,' he repeats. Sweat is dripping off him. Wibbly-wobbly jelly in the sun.

'You couldn't let her sleep down here?' says Uncle Nick, again changing Stevie's nappy. 'Her hips don't...'

'Lie,' butts in Auntie Gina, loudly and abruptly enough for Mum to spit gin right into her face.

'My eyes,' cries Auntie Gina waving her hands around, her eyes closed. It's like the impression she does of Nan behind her back as Nan couldn't see too well. She won't see any better underground either I suppose.

No one steps into help. Mum is still coughing. Uncle Nick rubs her back. He was rubbing her front when I caught them last month. Another secret I was told to keep. He claimed to have healing hands. Maybe I'll ask him to help out with Nan.

'Help me! My Christin' eyes!' yells Auntie Gina again, blindly waving. She's always bringing up Christ and Jesus and Jesus Christ. I have even heard her call for Jesus Fucking Christ but I don't know if they are the same person. Whoever it is doesn't seem to help. But again she is asking. Loudly.

'She's choking to death, G,' says Uncle Nick, attending to Mum. Uncle Nick always calls her G. For Gina. I once tried that. Mum and Dad told me not to.

'If I wasn't blind, I'd swing for you,' says Auntie G.

Dad still looks pale and sweaty so I grab a babywipe off the floor and pass it to Auntie Gina. She grabs it off me. I want to tell her to use the clean side but I'm too late. She smears Stevie's poo across her face and eyes, giving her a weird green complexion and horrified look on her face. Kinda like the one Dad and Mum had earlier when planting Nan.

Auntie Gina blinks through the mess, one eyelash stuck to the babywipe and the other half-ripped from her face. She has two sets of eyelashes. Maybe you grow a second set when you are an adult. Like the forest of hair growing from Dad and Uncle Nick's ears and nose.

Auntie Gina's mouth is open to scream but nothing comes out.

Mum has stopped coughing but Uncle Nick's rubbing continues. She breaks free of his healing hands—they worked again!—and returns with a towel. Clean. On both sides.

Mum and Dad are always wiping up after Nan. Crumbs and spilled tea. Then Toby's blood after Nan hit him with her walking stick. They buried Toby in the back garden too. I sat on the window upstairs and watched Dad do it. The hole was smaller than Nan's. Toby was old too. I am still waiting for him to grow.

Auntie Gina is looking at me strangely now. Her face is two different colours, the area around her eyes as white as a ghost while the rest remains deep brown. She looks like a panda. An angry panda.

Mum tells me to apologise. I explain I was only trying to help.

'I know that sweetie, but whenever we make mistakes we should apologise.'

I don't like to say sorry. It makes me feel bad. I was only trying to help.

'I tried to apologise to Nan, but...'

'That's enough of that,' cuts in Dad who rushes in and picks me up. Suddenly I am up high. I can feel Dad's sweaty palms through my clothes. What I was going to say is lost as if abandoned on the floor.

'She's sorry, aren't you, honey,' says Dad, staring at me with wide, scary eyes. He always looks at me that way when he wants me to repeat his words.

'I am sorry, Auntie Gina,' I say, looking down on her now, her blonde hair parted up top. It seems to come out of her head dark and then gets scared and loses colour. I wonder if that is what will happen with my hair too. I hope not. I like it brown.

'It's okay,' mumbles Auntie Gina, wiping at her eyes again. I don't think she means it.

'This is meant to be her party, remember,' says Uncle Nick. 'Do we wake her, or what?'

'We are not waking an old woman,' says Mum.

Dad nods so vigorously I shake in his arms making me involuntarily nod too. Like I am his puppet.

'She's bound to wake with all this racket,' says Uncle Nick, grabbing a handful of crisps from the bowl. Cheese and Onion. Ughhh.

'She couldn't hear the Grim Reaper if he came knocking,' says Auntie Gina. Normally Mum would tell her off. Auntie Gina is always saying things that they don't like.

'What?' says Auntie Gina, hanging out the front window puffing smoke that trails back inside the house. It smells horrible. 'You are not going to respond to that?'

Mum and Dad stay quiet. They look at each other again. It's not a look of love. It looks like discomfort. Maybe because Nan is outside and not upstairs. Maybe they are waiting to surprise them with what they have done. Or just wait 'til she sprouts like Mum's roses in Spring.

It is Auntie Gina's turn to look at Uncle Nick. She is frowning. The wrinkles make her look like one of those St Bernard dogs on TV. They are cuddly. Auntie Gina is not cuddly. Still they stare. Adults are always staring at each other without saying anything. I like staring contests but adults never announce them. They just have them.

Uncle Nick shrugs. He has bits of crisps in his beard. Mum doesn't like it. Dad says that Uncle Nick needs as much protection from Auntie Gina's cold heart as he can get.

'Really?' says Auntie Gina, 'Normally you would be all over that like shit off a shovel.'

Mum and Dad look at me. 'Shit'. A bad word. They don't tell me to cover my ears. They don't tell Auntie Gina off. They let that go too. Maybe all rules are out the window for Nan's birthday. Certainly the one about not leaving toys at the top of the stairs is anyway.

Uncle Nick wants to go upstairs. To say hello at least. Auntie G *agrees*. She wants to get it over with and get Stevie into the car before he wakes from his food coma. Half an hour peace without his bloody crying. She does as much crying as he does.

My parents refuse. Mum takes me upstairs and puts me in my room. I'm to stay there. I don't want to stay there. I haven't done anything wrong. Mum tells me I will go on the naughty step but I don't believe her. They didn't put me on the naughty step after what I did to Nan after all. I think this but all that comes out are tears. Mum tells me to stay inside and closes the door. I stand in the middle of the room crying. Tears rarely work these days. I am a 'big girl' apparently. I hear her dash across the hallway. That means that she isn't outside the door so...

I open the door. The hallway is empty. I walk along it wondering what I will do if I run into Mum. I think about going into Mum and Dad's room to jump on the bed for something to do but as I reach the door I see Mum in the spare room. Nan's room when she stays. She is pulling on one of Nan's old dresses, wrestling it over her head and down over her own. She must be cold. Then she grabs Nan's blonde wig from the plastic head that sits on the dresser, the one I am afraid of, the one that seems to stare at me anytime I pass by. She puts it on. She doesn't look much like Nan but it reminds me of the balloon and what happened. I got blamed. But Mum popped it, not me.

'Where's your Mum?' asks Uncle Nick with that smile he always has when discussing Mum. As if the thought of her makes him happy. Like Smarties do for me. They have come up the stairs and are now in the hallway.

Dad rushes forward and tries to stop my arm but it flashes towards Nan's room and the bed that Mum has just dived into. I tell Uncle Nick that she is over there. I don't say under the covers or in the wig.

Uncle Nick reaches the door just as Mum has settled in for a sleep.

Dad interrupts. 'She must be in the ensuite.'

'Why not use the big one?' asks Uncle Nick. He always questions Dad. Like they are rivals. I have one too. Tara O'Brien in my class. She is always showing off. This week it was the fact that her Dad has invited her out to Spain for the holidays. With another woman. According to Rachel's Mum it's some skanky bitch—another bad word—whose fanny is like a wizard's sleeve apparently. Which seems cool. I've always wanted to be a magician.

'Time of the month,' says Dad.

I ask Dad what he means. He looks to Uncle Nick and again they exchange this weird look like they want the other one to speak. This time no one speaks. They just go to leave the room, pulling me along.

'Happy birthday, Mum,' says Uncle Nick, tapping the bed.

It's not Mum's birthday for another three months but I don't say anything. It nice of Uncle Nick. I wish people would wish me happy birthday more often.

I was going to sing 'Happy Birthday' to Nan and give her the balloon with 75 on it. Even though I wanted to keep it.

Mum insisted I do it at the top of the stairs. Where my toys were scattered around. We had snuck up on her. Even though Nan can't hear well anymore. I was about to start when Mum popped the balloon. Nan stepped on some toys. Then fell. All the way to the bottom.

Uncle Nick and Auntie Gina don't stay around for long after. Just long enough to get Baby Stevie out of my old cot in the back room and Auntie Gina to finish another smoke. She doesn't like to smoke when she drives. It's dangerous for her health, she laughs. I don't get the joke.

About five minutes after they leave Mum is back downstairs. She isn't in Nan's dress and wig any longer. She doesn't look like she has had any sleep.

I am left alone to play. I try to involve Mum and Dad but they are busy. In separate rooms. When one enters, the other leaves. As if they are playing Tag by sight. Silly adults.

Dinner is pizza. Only I sit at the table. Mum leaves the kitchen after making sure I cool mine down. They don't usually allow me to but I take my dinner into the living room and get Dad to put on some cartoons. He does. This is great. They are letting me do anything I want. I eat the pizza. Dad drinks his special brown drink that makes my eyes water. I can hear Mum shuffling around upstairs. Maybe she is cleaning the house. I don't want to go up in case she asks me to help. I'll stick with the cartoons.

I watch so many I lose count. My eyes get tired. Normally they tell me to go to bed but Dad is slumped on the sofa staring straight ahead. Not at me or the TV. His eyes are like Nan's were.

She was still speaking when I got to the bottom of the stairs. Something about trying to kill. I didn't get the last part but there were some bad words involved. Mum pulled me out of the way as Dad used pillows to try and comfort her. One at the front and one at the back.

Mum and Dad were also using bad words. Mum was crying about what happened to Toby. They talked about stopping this and calling an ambulance but apparently it was too late for that. Nan must have been in a bad way. Her arms were flopping from side to side quite violently. Like one of Tina's seizures that makes Mr Yarrop order us all to the side of the room.

But instead of putting Nan on her side like Mr Yarrop does to Tina, Dad just pressed on the cushions harder. Until Nan calmed down. Unlike Mum and Dad.

I want to say sorry about the toys being at the top of the stairs where they shouldn't have been. I don't remember putting them there.

When Dad took away the pillow her eyes were like his are now. Staring. I touch his leg. His head swivels around towards me. He isn't like Nan. He doesn't smile. It makes me scared. I miss his smile.

I go upstairs to Mum. She is packing Nan's clothes into a bag. Probably to keep safe until she returns.

Mum tells me to go to bed. I ask her to read me a story. She tells me to ask Dad as all he is doing is drinking. He might even end up in a hole too, she mutters as I leave.

I ask Dad. He tells me to ask Mum.

I go to bed without a story.

Tomorrow I'll see if Nan has sprouted. If not I'll water her. I might even ask Mr Yarrop what the best way to grow a Nan is.

I like telling him about my weekends.

James Delargy

James Delargy was born and raised in Ireland but lived in South Africa, Australia and Scotland, before ending up in semi-rural England where he now lives.

He incorporates this diverse knowledge of towns, cities, landscape and culture picked up on his travels into his writing. He would like to complete a round-the-world series of novels (if only for the chance to indulge in more on-the-ground research).

His debut thriller, 55, was published in April 2019 by Simon & Schuster and has been sold to 21 territories to date.

@jdelargyauthor

Jamesdelargy.com

https://www.amazon.co.uk/dp/B07HFFT35H/

SHADOW

Kate Simants

My god though, the state of you now.

I move my hand over towards yours, throwing a glance at the guard enforcing the no-touching rule. He's looking the other way, shouting out to the room that visiting time is nearly over. You didn't recognise me when I came in, your eyes moving around my face like you were scanning an unfamiliar room. You haven't said a word—they told me you're not talking much. But I'd hoped you'd take my hand. I thought about it on the way here, the way your thumb used to move instinctively to stroke the stump of my missing little finger.

You keep your head down, flinching at the guard's voice as if every word is levelled right at your ear. And I'm not going to say it, but it's funny, in a way, after everything you said about how people never change. How I'd never change.

Because *you've* changed. We both have. Strange how things work out.

You can't even meet my eye. I made sure I'd be early enough to change out of my uniform before I got here because last time the sight of it made you cry. You wouldn't even sit at the table with me. Not that I'm surprised—I don't suppose I'd be a great fan of the police if I was in your shoes. But it was more than that, wasn't it? It was the reminder of how wrong you were about me. How different I am.

The thing was, after we found each other, I didn't really want to change. I wanted everything to stay the same. My days before you moved to the village were very long, and very empty, and when you arrived it felt like the sun had come out for the very first time. You saw my home-cut hair and the way my third-hand jeans were shiny with age. That first day, I know you saw the split in my lip I'd got from my dad the night before, and the blue-green swell that my brother put on my jaw. But you pretended you didn't see it at all.

You found me at the bus stop. Do you remember? The one up at the top estate, the other end of the village from the beautiful old house your family had just bought. The other end of the universe, the way it seemed to me.

I saw you coming and I stopped swinging my legs and just stared. I'd never seen anyone like you—it was as if you were lit up from the inside. That polished black leather jacket, even though you were only eleven. That sheet of white gold hair. To an eight-year-old truant—the fourth of six, invisible to even his own parents in the sobriety of daytime—your gaze speared me like a javelin through the chest. I loved you from that second, did you know? I did. But I ran away, terrified.

You didn't give up, though. You came looking for me. I didn't know why, back then. Didn't realise that in your world, where everyone was as luminous as you, I was the thing you were missing, the comparison you craved. A dark point to offset the brilliance. A shadow.

In the woods out the back of what had once been my grandad's barn, I had a den. Hidden from view, so you must have followed me there. I was collecting stones to make a path, only using my left hand because of what my brother had done to my finger. There was the snap of a branch and I saw you crouched there. Glowing, a smile on your face like you'd never been hurt.

I ran, again. But the next day, at the entrance to the den there was a little medical kit waiting for me. And after I'd opened it up, laying out the bandage and the wipes and latex gloves like a discovery of precious stones, out you crept. Palms up, eyes on mine.

Don't run away, was what you said. *I just want to help.* Your voice like the whisper of leaves.

So I relented. You moved slowly, edging closer, as if you were trying to catch a squirrel. You held out your hand for my injured one, and when we connected your touch was like an infusion, even through the pain. I watched your face as you peeled off the bit of dishcloth I'd tried to tie around it, and even though you recoiled when you saw what was underneath, when you smelt the decay that would have claimed my whole hand if you hadn't helped – it was only for a moment. When you looked up, the disgust was gone, a passing cloud.

Haven't you been to the doctor?

I hadn't.

Isn't there anyone at home to take you?

There wasn't.

Did—did someone do this on purpose?

I didn't reply to that either. But you already knew the answer.

You cocked your head. *Would you like me to look after you?*

I was eight years old. I didn't know what I was agreeing to.

Did you?

We went everywhere together after that, for a long time. Years. You spoke for me. You stuck up for me. Being with you made me untouchable at school, though no-one could understand what you saw in me.

Your parents wouldn't let me though your door but the painted playhouse in that forgotten corner of your enormous garden was my sanctuary. *You can live here forever*, you said, that one afternoon. Do you remember? But I was eleven myself by then, and I already had my plans. I'd told them to you, many times— how I'd be a police officer, with my own flat and my own car. So I thought you were joking, and I laughed.

That was the first time you hit me. You started crying before I did. You went white, eyes wide, saying how sorry you were, more shocked at what you'd done than I was. *I just don't want to lose you*, was what you said, your arms around me, trembling. *I just want to know you'll always be where I can find you.*

And yes, these days I might have my own home where the locks are on the inside, and my own fridge full of food that hasn't been scraped into bags for me, but there was never any cruelty in what you did, was there? Even when you took the top of my bad finger off, you did it with love.

I lift my hand to touch your hair, wondering at the lost lustre of it, every strand dull like a dead forest. *You'll always be right where I can find you,* I repeat under my breath. Your words. You look up, towards me but still not all the way, nothing but a medicated haze behind your eyes, as if you'd forgotten I was there. You open your mouth to say something, but then the guard is right next to us.

'I said no *touching,*' he barks, and you draw your head away from my reach. Obedient, the way I used to be, back when everything was just the way we wanted it. Until you met that other girl.

One morning when I'd spent the night in the little wooden playhouse, she came out of your house and across the lawn with you. She was dressed the same as you, ready for the fancy new high school you attended after your parents had decided the local one wasn't good enough. I remember the way my heart soared when I saw you, your hair shorter by then and your skirt too, your lovely legs sleek beneath the bouncing hem of your kilt, but then I saw her, trotting along beside you. I bolted for the flimsy door. But you had locked me in—when had you started doing that?—and there was nowhere to hide. You brought me out to show to her, like I was your pet. She'd brought food, but it was wrong. I could see from the way she was holding it. Something too soft about it. Too liquid.

We mustn't be ungrateful, you told me. So I put my hand out for the bag, because I wasn't ungrateful.

You must eat now, because you're hungry, aren't you?

I shook my head.

We mustn't tell lies, you said. So I did what you said. She watched, mouth agape, as you fed me.

123

Later, when you'd gone, I ran all the way back to my den, overgrown and forgotten by then, and I dropped to my knees and vomited until there was nothing but bile.

Did you wonder what had happened to me, after that? Or did you forget me? Because I didn't forget you. I watched for you, to see if you'd come to find me. Out of sight, I waited at the bus stop, and by the playhouse, and near the old den. But you didn't come.

Not even when my brother died. Did you even know?

Not even when the house burned down.

You outgrew what we had. But it was never going to work that way for me. That's the thing with shadows, I suppose. They need light to cast them. It's not like I had a choice.

So even though you never looked for me, I came to you. I saw you every day, just enough to feel your sunshine on my face. You finished at that school, and went to a college in the city for sixth form. That girl went there, too. When you went to university I lost sight of you for a little while, and again when the two of you moved to your flat in Cambridge. But I didn't lose you for long. Sure, being on the force has helped. Though it has to be said, someone like you would never be too hard to find.

Someone like you were, at least. After sentencing, you spent your first three months in a secure hospital, on twenty-four hour watch. Your parents campaigned for you. But no-one else went in or out of the flat that night, did they? No-one left a trace. It was only you and her there. And money can't buy an alibi.

We have only a couple of minutes left. I shift over a little closer, filling up on you now, soaking up what's left of your radiance. Your eyes find mine fully for the first time since I got here, and slowly they start to narrow, focusing. You draw back, your hands start to brace against the edge of the table. Your mouth starts to move.

Shhh, I tell you. I know what you're going to say. But look—I just don't think you really mean it, do you?

Because if you really had cared about her, if you'd wanted to keep her safe, wouldn't you have made sure? That window wasn't even locked. Even the CCTV system, bought because you were so paranoid you were being followed, could have been set up by a child. Was your heart really in it? Because it felt like you were waiting for me. Inviting me in. Resetting the footage that night took me minutes.

She was already fast asleep when I went into her room. I watched her for a little while. I crouched by her bed. I smelt her warm breath. And then I came to find you.

The jury didn't believe that you had no memory of it. And OK, I'll admit that the time you spent on the stand was hard for me to watch because I could see their folded arms, the shaking of their heads when you said you didn't know what had happened, that you had gone to bed that night and woken late the next morning, oblivious of what you'd done, and no idea how you'd broken your little finger. But snapping it like that would have caused you too much pain, if I'd kept you awake. So I chose the lesser of two evils. It was only a little injection. You didn't even feel it.

Her, though: I wanted her to feel everything. Every point of pressure around her throat, right to the end. Hard enough to leave dark marks like a necklace. Nine prints, because of your poor, injured finger.

Chairs start to scrape back—the warden says it's time. I take one last look at you, spread my hands flat on the table. Then I get up to go.

Seeing my hands, you suddenly jolt back. You reach out for my hand, snatching it near. Like a spell has broken, fully conscious now you pass your thumb over the stump of my little finger. You look up at me, horror darkening your face.

You, you say.

And I smile. I'd forgotten what it is to be truly seen.

Me, I agree. And I turn and walk away, leaving you screaming.

When the light is gone, the shadows can stretch out in the dark.

Kate Simants

Kate Simants spent several years as an investigative TV journalist, for both Channel 4 and the BBC. She specialised in police undercover work, contributing to various investigations and exposés from fraudulent witchdoctors to abuse in children's homes.

Since leaving the media, Kate has focused on fiction. Her debut novel LOCK ME IN was shortlisted for a CWA Debut Dagger, and she won the UEA Literary Festival scholarship to study for an MA in Crime Fiction. Under its previous title of THE KNOCKS, A RUINED GIRL won the 2019 Bath Novel Award, published by Viper in August 2020. Kate lives near Bristol with her family.

@katesboat

https://amzn.to/3bROrEf for Lock Me In

https://amzn.to/2X14yLM for A Ruined Girl

AUTHOR LINKS

Adam Southward

@adamsouthward

https://www.amazon.co.uk/Adam-Southward/e/B07NQNXLLG/

Dominic Nolan

@NolanDom

https://www.amazon.co.uk/Dominic-Nolan/e/B07QBMZ5T4

Elle Croft

@elle_croft

https://amzn.to/2X3vOsO

S R Masters

@srmastersauthor.

www.sr-masters.com

https://www.amazon.co.uk/Killer-You-Know-Original-gripping/dp/0751570362/ref=tmm_pap_swatch_0?_encoding=UTF8&qid=1585823497&sr=8-1

Phoebe Morgan

@Phoebe_A_Morgan

https://www.amazon.co.uk/Phoebe-Morgan/e/B0735BVTRG/ref=dp_byline_cont_ebooks_1

N J Mackay

@NikiMackayBooks

https://www.amazon.co.uk/Niki-Mackay/e/B079YR5742?ref_=dbs_p_ebk_r00_abau_000000

Victoria Selman

@VictoriaSelman

http://www.victoriaselmanauthor.com/

https://www.amazon.co.uk/Victoria-Selman/e/B07HX4NK9Y/ref=dp_byline_cont_ebooks_1

Rachael Blok

@MsRachaelBlok

rachaelblok.com

https://www.amazon.co.uk/Rachael-Blok/e/B07HJ5MDSB?ref=sr_ntt_srch_lnk_1&qid=1586074405&sr=8-1

Heather Critchlow

@h_critchlow

www.heathercritchlow.com

Jo Furniss

@Jo_Furniss

www.jofurniss.com

www.facebook.com/JoFurnissAuthor/

Instagram @jofurnissauthor.

https://www.amazon.co.uk/Jo-Furniss/e/B06X6H82N3/ref=dp_byline_cont_ebooks_1

Robert Scragg

@robert_scragg

www.robertscragg.com

https://www.amazon.co.uk/Robert-Scragg/e/B075GKQLPC/
ref=dp_byline_cont_ebooks_1

Clare Empson

@ClareEmpson2

https://www.amazon.co.uk/Clare-Empson/e/B07GBXNM9G?
ref=sr_ntt_srch_lnk_1&qid=1586187043&sr=8-1

James Delargy

@jdelargyauthor

Jamesdelargy.com

https://www.amazon.co.uk/dp/B07HFFT35H/

Kate Simants

@katesboat

https://amzn.to/3bROrEf for Lock Me In

https://amzn.to/2X14yLM for A Ruined Girl

Printed in Great Britain
by Amazon